*"I am suspended . . .
Now is nothing, a void . . .*

**"When there are no more shadows, then
one is ready, one no longer weaves a line
to cast into the future. One of the shadows
in that future must be myself; sometimes
it seems to turn to gaze back at me, to
reach out and lay a hand on me that I can
feel in a way that no words have been
invented to describe. I reached out to myself
as a child, dancing at the edge of the lava
fields, touched the child I was, reassured
the child I was. Did I as child sense a shadow
from the future? I don't know.**

**"And that's the final frustration: we don't
know; we can't be certain; there is no proof."**

Books by Kate Wilhelm

City of Cain
The Clewiston Test
Fault Lines
The Infinity Box
Juniper Time
Margaret and I
Where Late the Sweet Birds Sang

Published by TIMESCAPE/POCKET BOOKS

KATE WILHELM
FAULT LINES

A TIMESCAPE BOOK
PUBLISHED BY POCKET BOOKS NEW YORK

A Timescape Book published by
POCKET BOOKS, a Simon & Schuster division of
GULF & WESTERN CORPORATION
1230 Avenue of the Americas, New York, N.Y. 10020

ISBN: 0-671-42425-4

First Pocket Books printing September, 1978

10 9 8 7 6 5 4 3 2

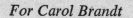

For Carol Brandt

FAULT LINES

1

Eight miles from the center of San Francisco there is a fracture in the earth's crust—the San Andreas Fault. The fault line is six hundred fifty miles long and thirty miles deep and the mass on the west of it wants to slide northward while the land on the east tries to drift south. About fourteen miles to the east is the Hayward Fault. Between the two zones and on the outer sides of them are many lesser faults, sometimes paralleling them, sometimes radiating out from them, and in this area the land lies in a state of disequilibrium; it can find relief from the inexorable pressure of opposing forces only through violent movement.

That is the beginning of an article I have been reading in manuscript. I paraphrase, of course; I didn't memorize it. The author lives in Chicago and has knowledge about earthquakes and faults and fracture zones from an intensive education that has spanned fifteen years of college life. I had already decided to return the article before I came out here to the shore. Facts, facts, facts, and no truth. No real truth.

You are awakened by the sound of china jiggling softly, as if someone has bumped into the cabinet, set the shelves in motion, or as if a ghostly pressure is signaling its arrival. There is a deeper sound, booted feet running across the wide porch, a cracking noise as something hits and passes through the carved redwood door; inside the house the pressure expands to fill all available space, as gas does in a container. It races across the floor, brushing the walls, rearranging pictures, setting the chandelier adance, stirring the ashes in the fireplace, as if searching for a scrap of paper inadvertently burned. The deep sharp breaking, cracking noise is everywhere, yet is without a source. In the basement a beam groans, in the attic rafters twist and unburden themselves of a decade's collection of dust. In the kitchen crockery slides on Formica surfaces; copper pots on the chimney wall beat a tattoo; in the bathroom the door of the medicine cabinet flies open, mouthwash slides out and crashes into the sink, and the fragrance of mint is in the air. Your bed rocks and you wonder why babies find this soothing, and all the while you are counting: . . . 27 hippopotamus, 28 hippopotamus . . . 75 hippopotamus . . . There is a rifle crack on the terrace—one of the French doors has broken again. You count because you believe, as everyone else does, that if the earth relieves itself of the unbearable tensions by shivering and trembling for a minute or two the real quake won't come . . . 87 hippopotamus . . .

Sometimes it happens too fast to count, and that's how it was this time. I came wide awake with the roar and thunder still in my head, reverberating in my bones, and I knew. Earthquake, I thought, almost deliberately; I should get out of bed, stand in the doorway, or get under the bed, or run out into the open. I should not simply lie here. But my bed was shaking, and I clung to it, and around me the house was breaking up. I could hear glass shattering, wood snapping and groaning. I started to roll over, thinking of open ground away from the beams and roof; before I could leave it, the bed dropped, and the crashes were very close and sharp. The bed came to rest at an angle, but something had fallen on top of me and I was wedged in place. I found that I was holding my breath, that I was light-headed from holding my breath so long, and I let it go. The bed shuddered once, twice more. Everything became still again. It was over.

If I had managed to get up, I realized, I probably would have been killed when the house fell. I was content to lie without movement, waiting for terror and nausea to subside, recognizing them both as strange and somewhat distant feelings that were mine and yet apart from me. At last I felt I should do something else, and I tried to rise, and found that I could not move. The bed that had saved my life now held me fast, and I could not move at all.

I tried each muscle in turn, following the relaxation method in which you first tense and then relax yourself, starting with the left toe, then the right, the left calf, right, left thigh . . . Always before, somewhere between the abdominal group and the fingers I fell asleep. I can tense and relax all my muscles now, but I can't lift my feet or raise my hands, or roll over or turn my head. I am not really uncomfortable, lying on my stomach, nothing doubled under me, something on me that doesn't feel like a beam or a wall—perhaps the chaise turned over on me, and now, with the mattress below and the cushioned chaise above, I am like a salami in a sandwich, placed here without consent, helpless to protest. I am not hurt, I think, although I may be in a state of shock that has somehow severed my consciousness from the distress signals my body may be sending.

If you become lost in the woods, sit quietly and wait for help. Do not panic. Do not run. Help, I'm waiting for you! I am lying here quietly just waiting for you. I am lost, Help, even though there are no woods here.

I was holding my breath again, bracing myself for the aftershocks that would shake my house from its precarious perch, shake me with it into the sea, which sounded close enough now to indicate that my cliff had fallen to pieces on the beach. Even as I expelled my breath I thought of the earth gathering its forces to make the minor adjustments its new alignments demanded.

You ran away, I told myself severely, and this is what you deserve, instant punishment. You should have leveled with them, there were chances, plenty of opportunities, and you didn't have the guts to face them. I was listening to the sea again. Resolutely I forced myself instead to remember the chances I had passed up, when I could have faced the truth with my family and friends.

Dinner, ten of us in the dining room eating Dorrie's shrimp gumbo, home-made bread, home-grown salad, Tony's wine. Sometimes it was beans and rice, sometimes pot roast, occasionally chops, not often, not with ten or more to share them each night. We could almost manage the food bills, I thought, and tried not to think of the gallons of milk we drank each day, the gallons of coffee, tons of flour, sugar, butter. . . . I pulled away from the revolving thoughts, back to Kenneth.

". . . so I made Warren pull me along in the wagon and I snapped pictures of shoppers, passing cars, trolleys. It's amazing, you'll love it."

Kenneth has bushy hair, not quite black, tinged with gray now, but still out of control. He has a scar on his right cheek, from falling on a beer bottle when he was a child, and being afraid to go home until it was nearly healed, too late then for stitches. He is six feet tall, about one hundred eighty pounds. I can't visualize him scrunched down in a wagon, being pulled through town.

A lovely series of pictures passed through my mind, with text by Johnny Berio maybe. He does children very well. Johnny sent me an article once that was cut into narrow strips of text. So I wouldn't have to do it myself, his bitter little note said.

"You're not listening," Kenneth said, touching my hand.

"I am. A Child's Eye View of the World. It's a grand idea. I can hardly wait to see the pictures."

"Most of you wasn't listening," Kenneth said knowingly.

"It's frightening, looking at the world from only so high off the ground," Regina said, glancing at her son Brucie, who was playing with his shrimp, making his dinner of bread and butter and milk. He could do worse, I thought.

Homer began to tell about the school he had attended in Oklahoma—a corrugated shed with a tin roof where the temperature climbed high enough each afternoon to cook the goldfish in the aquarium.

"Why did they have an aquarium in there if it got that hot?" Katherine asked.

"So we could take pictures of it and send it to our congressman periodically."

"Oh. Is it true that Indians used to be afraid of blondes and find them irresistible?" Katherine is blond.

"Sure. Blondes, redheads, brunettes, brownettes, yellow gals, black gals, you name it."

She blushed and ducked her head.

"Thought I might start painting the trim, if that's all right," Jepson Dollard said. He is Dorrie's friend who moved in at her invitation five years ago and stayed. We don't pay him anything, can't afford to pay him, but he stays anyway and does things. He tends the salad garden, and paints the trim, and fixes the dishwasher or oven or whatever goes wrong, and he watches Dorrie with soft eyes and teaches Brucie about carving, and sometimes goes fishing and provides us with fish for a month. He is about sixty, retired, with a small pension, and wants to call my house home. He has his meals with us, the family, but if there is company he vanishes. I wish he would fix the plaster in the dining room, but I can't ask him to.

"What's wrong?" Kenneth asked me softly while Homer told another story about an archaeologist who dug up bits of Sears Roebuck pottery and pieced them together night after night while the Indians sat in a circle watching silently, solemnly.

I patted Kenneth's hand and turned my attention to Warren, who never took his eyes off Kenneth. Warren is my great-nephew. Warren has the same hungry, yearning look that seems to run in my family, but he doesn't want gold, he wants to be Kenneth Cruze the world-renown photographer, or if not be Kenneth, at least be near him at all times. Kenneth is kind to him although the boy must nearly drive him crazy.

"Jack Black called," Dorrie said, "and he'll call back. I told him to drop a note, but it's urgent, he has to tell you himself."

I groaned. Jackson Black is screwy, with a new conspiracy theory each week, new evidence of UFOs each month, new proof that the FBI, CIA, NSA, and half a dozen municipal police forces are having him followed. He thinks he can get an article in the magazine if only he can write it smoothly enough, with enough elegance to suit me, and enough hard evidence to suit the lawyers he knows are hovering in the wings waiting for him to slip up so they can sentence him to jail forever.

Everything was unnaturally sharp—the ring of silver, the tinkling of ice in glasses, ruby wine by candlelight, the white tablecloth that is getting so threadbare that Dorrie has to place the flowers in strategic spots, hide the thin places with the bread board and self-adhering daisies, the murmur of voices and the laughter as Homer finished his story about the archaeologist and his tape-recordings of ancient tribal chants that translated to something like Higgeldy piggeldy worms are so wiggeldy.

Homer is writing a suspense novel set in Oklahoma on

his reservation, with a Kiowa detective using his own inscrutable methods to uncover the criminal. It will sell to Hollywood and make him rich and I wonder if the money will kill him. I almost wish he had not shown me the chapters, had not outlined it for me, had not come to me in the first place. Homer is broad and heavy and laughs easily, but his eyes do not laugh. Sometimes late at night I can hear his typewriter tapping away, then nothing, and often during those times of silence I find him stalking shadows through my house, perhaps the ghosts of my parents, or their parents.

"I can't do it," he says then, despair and hopelessness thickening his voice. "It's no good."

"You're stuck, right? Let's have a look." And we go to my study, my father's old study, and sit before the fireplace, where I read the pages while he squirms and mutters evil things.

Homer knows many things I don't know and can't know because my brain won't admit that my eyes can see what his eyes see. We meet and talk in a narrow area where his reality and mine touch.

The twins, Karen and Katherine, cleared the table and brought a bowl of fruit and a plate of cookies, and coffee. The phone rang and Regina left and didn't return. Her ex-husband threatens her with all sorts of terrible things—he will take Brucie away from her, he will make her pay his doctor bills, he wants the car back and is going to send someone after it. . . . I wish she would call the police and have him arrested, but she won't, and she tries to hide the fact that she is afraid of him, for Brucie more than herself. Brucie knows and he pretends he doesn't and it is all very unpleasant, but I can't tell them to leave. She is Gloria Woodson's daughter and will have a home with me as long as she wants it, as long as I have a home.

Kenneth brought his pictures to the study and I looked at them with him, with Warren hovering in the background. "They're fantastic," I said, and it was true. They are marvelous, and frightening. The world the child sees is different, a scary world of distorted people that changes as adults sit down, or stand up, that makes common buildings with short flights of stairs become imposing, looming structures that threaten to smother a small child. Hallways become nightmares of shadows and distances that seem endless. That explains our own nightmares a bit, I thought,

staring down the hallway of the public library that I knew
so well, but that was now strange and menacing, caught
from this angle, three feet from the floor.

"They are very good," I said finally, "better than I
imagined they would be. What a horrible world!"

"The little bastards accept it all right," Kenneth said
cheerfully. "But it reawakens something that's been dor-
mant awhile, doesn't it?"

I could only nod, unable to shrug away the pictures and
the strange world children view. I could see how an issue
could be shaped around his photographs. The *Golden
Gate Review* is a literary magazine, and I seldom use any
illustrations, but Kenneth Cruze doesn't do illustrations, he
reveals our world as surely as any poet or prose writer,
and the impact of his photographs is immediate and vis-
ceral.

He wanted me to say, I'll buy them, we'll use them in
the Christmas issue, or early spring, or something. He
waited. He could never say will you take them, or make
any move to indicate that he wanted me to buy his
pictures. I stared at them until they blurred, and finally
mumbled, "I can't buy anything right now, or I would
take them."

The tension vanished and Kenneth laughed and began
to gather them together once more. "I thought you didn't
like them," he said. Everyone else knows he is a genius,
but Kenneth is always surprised again when others are
forced to admit to seeing his visions frozen in photographs. "Actually the series isn't quite finished yet. There
are other things I want to do like this, amusement parks,
animals, you know, all the usual children's fun things."

I nodded, and then, aware that the implications of what
I had said would finally surface and he would start asking
me questions, I fled to my room. After a few moments
Dorrie followed.

"Can you tell me what's wrong?" she asked.

I was sitting before the fireplace, where no fire burned
that pleasant evening. I shook my head. "The colonel is
dying. He didn't know me when I went to visit."

She nodded and sat down also. "Warren and the girls
are doing the dishes. It won't last long, but while it does I
intend to take advantage of their willingness to lend a
hand."

"I've been thinking, we should post rules—so many hours of labor in exchange for room and board."

Dorrie laughed and didn't comment. We talked easily, as old friends, with no strain usually, but that night I had something to hide and she sensed it, and the tension that had evaporated downstairs had followed me upstairs. That was when I decided to go away for a few days, to go to the beach house alone to think.

"I have to get away," I said. "There's trouble with circulation, they want some changes in format, and I have to be alone to think."

Dorrie nodded. We shared almost everything except the magazine, and very early she had told me she would stay out of that. She was a poor reader, found no pleasure in books or articles or stories. She liked to look at the pictures, she said, and that was all.

"Don't tell anyone where I've gone, okay? I don't want company at all."

"Not even Mr. Kodel?"

I shook my head. Maybe that was the reason I kept putting him off, I thought. Dorrie called him Mr. Kodel and he called her Miss Holstead. None of my other friends considered her a maid, or paid companion, or servant, and in fact she was not—she is a partner—but Tony calls her Miss Holstead and is too polite to her, too distant, and she is stiff and formal with him.

"And if cra—if Louis comes or sends flowers, don't accept them. Tell him I've developed a terrible allergy or something, that they might kill me. And don't tell him anything else at all." He might decide to come looking for me, and I couldn't bear another scene with him.

And so, instead of facing them, explaining to them my situation, and consequently their situation also, I had ducked out. You're too stubborn, Emily, I told myself sternly; you're too proud to ask for help and advice, you've got to go it alone. Well, you're alone, I said, as tight in here as the last pickle packed in the jar, and God knows how long it will be before someone comes to rescue you since you purposely didn't tell anyone you were coming out here except Dorrie, and she is sound asleep. Even then I didn't believe the earthquake had been a major one. It was in the wrong place, too far from the San Andreas Fault. I tried to draw comfort from visualizing Dorrie sleeping peacefully, my great-nieces, my great-nephew,

Kenneth, Homer, the others who shared my house, all sleeping quietly, freed for the night from whatever problems pursued them by day.

"Leave her be. She's dancing to celebrate life."

Like a shock of ice water, I suddenly hear my father's voice, which I didn't hear at the time, saying words that I have never remembered in all these years until now.

My father was a slender tough man. He was only five feet six and looked frail, but he never tired, never complained, never became ill from anything until he died of a sudden massive coronary. I wonder if he had had minor heart ailments for years, and simply paid no attention, or denied them, or pretended that by an act of will he could overcome even a faulty heart action. He was a geologist/teacher. By train, by automobile, by foot we had gone to Oregon, to the volcanic regions west of Bend.

"The wind and rain and snow loosen the rocks," he told me, "and eventually they come tumbling down the mountains and gather in the lowlands, where they keep getting added to year after year. Finally the weight and the friction on the material below . . . You know what friction is?" He rubbed my hands together until they became warm. "That's friction. Same thing happens to the rocks. They keep on getting rubbed together until they get hotter and hotter and all the time more's being added and the load gets heavier, and the pressure adds more heat. Finally the basalts start to melt and this molten material is lighter than all the stuff pressing down on it and it tries to rise. When it finds a weak place, it gushes out and we have a volcano."

Words, facts. Many of the facts long since invalidated.

The truth was the semiarid country around Bend, done in grays and browns as far as I could see eastward, the empty sky, and a steady hot wind that burned my face and brought tears to my eyes. We ascended the mountains once more, traveling on a gravel road that permitted two automobiles to pass only if the inside one stopped to hug the mountain long enough for the outside one to edge around it. It became cooler after a few minutes of climbing. The mountains smelled of earth and leaf mold, of recently melted snow, of spruce and pine trees and rock dust from the white stream gravel that had been crushed and spread on the roadbed. Father drove and Sandy, one

of his students who was always about in those years, sat
beside him in front, chewing his nails and staring out the
side window. He wanted to drive and made an uneasy
passenger. His name was Sanderling, he had been in
France and had been wounded and walked with a limp
that later became unnoticeable, but that year, 1915, he
limped badly and was very nervous. He set up camp later
that afternoon and early the next morning we hiked the
rest of the way. I walked behind Sandy and tried to imi-
tate his limp until my father swatted me sharply on the
bottom. I wasn't being maliciously cruel. I really wanted
to find out what it would be like to walk that way. Adults
always assume the worst motives for the actions of
children.

There was no demarcation zone. We were in dense
woods one moment, then left the trees, and stopped.
Spread out before us was a sea of lava. I felt as though
the air had been squeezed from my chest and I couldn't
draw in another breath. We were on a steep mountainside
and lava filled the entire valley, three thousand feet deep,
mile after mile, like a gigantic river of black sharp rocks
that wound among island hills.

"There's one of the cones," Father said, taking my arm,
turning me to face the right direction.

I saw a mountaintop spinning off into the sky, a red
plume of fire shooting hundreds of feet into the air, a
fountain of glowing red rocks bursting out from it in all
directions, filling the air with brilliance, kindling trees,
flaring them like torches, then swallowing them in the rush
of a red-gold river that raced through the valleys. I caught
my breath and there came a release; I spun around and
pivoted and threw my arms up and spun again and again.

"Leave her be. She's dancing to celebrate life."

I can see her now, a wild little girl, her hair in long pale
braids that hadn't been undone and brushed for days, that
were straggly and dirty with bits of leaves and twigs here
and there; dirt on her face, which was red from sun- and
wind-burn; dressed in her brother's trousers, which were
too long and too snug, but better than her own skirts
would have been, whirling about in a spontaneous dance
that had to be danced.

Sandy watched her warily for a long time after that,
certain that she had been temporarily crazed. She might
have been, I think, that little girl who knew no other way

to express the vastness of the emotions that gripped her that day. Strange, I think now, my father understood even if I never did until this moment. I feel almost as if I can reach out through, or around, time and touch that child, reassure her/me somehow that it is all right to dance, to feel overwhelmed by something that cannot be named or seen or described, but that is experienced as real and enduring forever.

We stayed in the lava fields for several days and then drove south once more and again left the automobile to hike through woods, this time to Crater Lake, where all the mountain except the southern exposure was still covered by icy snow. And that night my father told me a story.

"Thousands of years ago, long before the white men came to this country, the Klamath Indians lived here. They hunted and fished and traded with other Indians and were happy. They had many chiefs they paid homage to. One of them was Llao, chief of the world below. Llao lived under this mountain, Mount Mazama, but in those days there wasn't a lake on the top as there is today. There was just snow, like on all the other peaks. When the weather was clear the Indians could sometimes see Llao come up from his home and stand on Mount Mazama to look around. He was mighty, and black, and looked like a giant shadow against the snow."

My father paused for me to firm up the picture in my mind, but there was little need. I could see that great black shadow dancing on the snow. He went on.

"Now, farther south, about a hundred miles away on top of Mount Shasta lived another one of the Klamath chiefs. This one was Skell, chief of the world above. It made Skell furious that Llao came out from the world below as often as he did. One day they got into a fight that became a fierce war."

"Like the war Sandy was in?"

"Much worse than that," he said. "When men make wars, sometimes they make little craters; in a few years the craters get filled with earth again and you can't even tell where they were, but this lake was made ten thousand years ago, and it's as big now as it was then."

I nodded and he continued.

"Skell and Llao threw burning rocks at each other, and caused burning rivers to run out of the earth. They burned up the forests, and the earth shook for seven days and nights. There was so much dust and smoke in the air that in the daytime no light showed except the light of the burning forests and rocks and molten rivers. Whole hills were shaken down into plains, whole forests were consumed and the noise was so terrible that many of the Indians were made deaf by it. They tried to run away, but there seemed nowhere to go where the earth was not shaking and the air was not filled with smoke. Then finally Skell threw one last boulder so large and so hot that it burned the top off Mount Mazama and caused it to explode in one final eruption. This eruption was greater than everything that had gone before, and when it was over Llao was defeated. After Llao was banished back to the world below, Skell caused the rains to come to fill in the hole, and this lake is what remains today. There is no bottom that man has ever found." He paused while Sandy added sticks to the fire. Flares cracked like shots. "To this day you won't find any Klamath Indians who are willing to come up here," my father said. "This is sacred ground where Llao's ghost lives, cursed for all time by Skell."

It had grown very dark while he told his story; the small circle of light seemed to have drawn inward, the blackness beyond to have solidified, to have formed a wall that enclosed us and reflected back our feeble firelight, which didn't penetrate the darkness beyond at all.

"Lies," Sandy muttered. "Lies told by savages."

"Not lies," my father protested. "Superstitions aren't lies in any sense of the word. They simply didn't know any better and tried to account for the world and this strange happening in the best way they could."

My father went on to lecture about the importance of preserving local myths and legends without at the same time succumbing to the temptation to add any trace of them to the fund of real knowledge men of science were constantly building. I listened, no longer understanding, and stared at the solid wall that separated the blackness from us where we sat close together, sheltered by the circle of flickering light.

And I thought the Klamath Indians were right: beyond that wall the ghost of chief Llao walked without a sound, leaving no trace that we would ever see.

That was the happiest summer of my life. We roamed in the hills and mountains for weeks, my father working,

Sandy helping, both of them pointing out the world to me, explaining it in terms of pressures, of subterranean forces, sometimes forgetting me for hours at a time, when I was free to wade wild streams, pick up thunder eggs and bits of jade and pyrite, blood-red jasper and agates. I have a piece of water agate on my desk today, saved all these years, handled until it has been worn as smooth as a worked artifact.

My desk will be cleaned off finally. Dorrie will have her way and the top will gleam and show all the wood grain. The last time the desk was cleaned off was when we moved back into the house, twenty-nine years ago. I don't want to think about the house and what I'll have to do about it now.

"Write your memoirs," Jackie Wonder said to me last week. That isn't his name, but it fits in a way that his own probably does not. I can't remember his name. Perhaps he doesn't have a name, just a number, or not even that, just a designation: Mr. Owens's assistant. "Write your memoirs. I can guarantee that we'll publish them, in serial form if they're long enough."

I tried not to laugh. He couldn't guarantee his presence at the next coffee break.

Never trust a man who doesn't shave, who polishes his cheeks to a glossy pink and wears clothes out of the most recent issue of *Playboy*. Jackie Wonder is possibly twenty-five, fresh out of Harvard Business School with grades that put him in the top third of his class, with ties by marriage, or blood oath, or fraternity rites, to executives of one or two of the largest corporations. This year he is nameless—someone's assistant—but in ten years he will have his own office and assistant and no one will forget his name. He didn't choose to tell me; it was a committee decision to be carried out by one of the nameless ones.

"Is Stu Mitchell still here?" I asked.

"Yes, but . . ."

He didn't actually touch me in order to stop me, but he wanted to and at the last instant fear withdrew his hand and he followed me through the corridors to Stu's office. I had worked through Stu since the parent corporation had bought out the magazine. He was the only one I knew.

Stu Mitchell is in his early thirties and he won't go much further than he has already. He doesn't have the drive, or the ready answer, and he was probably ruined by working for a small independent electronics company that was absorbed by the corporation seven years ago. The corporation took him, also, but the ladder has ended here for him. His office doesn't even have a window, not a good sign.

"Emily, how great you look! Sit down. How are you?"

"What's this about creating a new image?"

"Oh. He's already told you?"

"Why didn't you tell me I was being fired?"

"Emily, you're not being fired! That's ridiculous! You've been with the magazine for twenty-nine years, and you're almost seventy years old. It's policy to retire at sixty-five or after twenty-five years of service. Even the highest executives retire. No one has singled you out for any extraordinary treatment. Mr. Owens is planning to have a dinner in your honor, a special issue devoted to you, the works. The company is very proud—"

"Shit! The colonel promised me when he sold the magazine I could retain my position as long as I want it. I don't want to retire!"

"But policy—"

"I'll see the colonel about policy!" We both knew that was meaningless. The colonel was too preoccupied with dying to care, even if he had retained any control, and he had not.

"Look, Emily, it won't do any good. The magazine's been losing money. We had Byerly Research do a demographic survey for us, and the consensus is that we need to revamp the magazine. Fewer sherry drinkers, more Harvey Wallbanger people. Younger people who are spending money for things our advertisers have to offer. You know how that goes. The magazine has always been too specialized, it needs a broader base to appeal to a wider market, a general market. If it can't show a profit, there's just no point in continuing it."

"Don't tell me about that survey. I saw it, remember. Byerly's methods are unreliable, they load their samples to prove whatever they have decided they need to prove. They can't even defend their own methods! They don't try!"

"Emily, advertisers have no problems with Byerly. They accept the findings. They need documentation to present to their own people—the officers of the companies, the boards of directors, stockholders . . ."

"But the numbers don't mean anything!"

"I'm afraid you simply don't understand modern statistical science."

"I understand that our magazine isn't losing money. We cut down on the year-end bonuses last year and didn't lose a cent of anyone's money. We're one of the few publications that haven't. And to hold our own in the middle of a depression is an accomplishment. Don't tell me what I don't understand."

"You don't understand the make-up of a corporation, Emily. The decision has been made. The magazine is going to be restyled completely, maybe even be renamed. It needs a new, modern image. And there's no appeal about the decision to retire employees after twenty-five years with the firm if they are over sixty-five."

I got up and went to the door. Jackie Wonder was still there. I had forgotten about him. "Is he going to be on the staff now?" Stu nodded. "You are right, Stu. I don't understand about corporate actions. I also don't understand all the chemical processes that take place in the decomposition of garbage. But I by God know it when I smell it!"

I didn't wait for an appointment with Mr. Owens. I checked out of my hotel, caught the next plane home, dismissed the taxi at the foot of the hill, and walked the rest of the way in a thin fog that was like sheer moist curtains, screening and softening harsh lines of walls and concrete buildings, diluting the effects of the streetlights, somehow muting the world to a more humane level.

I walked slowly, trying to think how I would tell those people whom I loved, who loved me, who shared my house, my life, shared everything with me. My mind kept veering away from them. There was no way I could tell them. Then I thought about my house.

2

In 1849 Hilliard Krump's mother and father and two sisters were killed by marauding Indians near Topeka, Kansas. Hilliard, the sole beneficiary of the estate of four hundred acres, sold his holdings to Samuel Larssen, married the youngest Larssen daughter, Geneva, and bought a rig to travel to the gold fields of California. Hilliard was twenty, Geneva sixteen. I have only my father's stories to guide me now; he had no pictures, nothing but his memory to call on. Hilliard was about his size, five six or so, slightly built, fair complexioned, as was Geneva, who was several inches taller and twenty pounds heavier than her husband.

They lived comfortably enough and he actually found gold within five years, and also in that time they had four children and went broke. Hilliard moved on to Montana, leaving his young family behind, and this time when he returned he had found copper. My father said Hilliard had a nose for minerals, he could smell gold, silver, copper, whatever he was looking for, and there could be something to this. Now Hilliard was wealthy; his copper claim was more extensive than the gold he had come upon earlier. He bought land in and around San Francisco, invested in a general store, bought his wife the finest linens, silver, china. But he couldn't make her happy. Geneva was unbearably homesick for the plains of Kansas.

It wasn't that she was a coward. She had proved her bravery several times over: during the trip to the coast through Indian country; when she stayed alone with the children and another on the way; in fact, by leaving her family in the first place when she was only sixteen. I imagine her and Hilliard loving their way West, laughing, playing, at times cowering in fear, clinging to each other while the nights made menacing sounds. If the journey could have continued forever, would she then have been happy? Only to travel toward, never to arrive, never to be disappointed by the destination, would that have satisfied her? My father has talked of their trip with respect and admiration. They were not part of a wagon train. Hilliard was too impatient for that. He was familiar with Kansas, from the plains to the foothills of the mountains, and needed no guide, and wanted none.

It was not fear that destroyed their marriage, it was the shock of the strange—future shock, not named, not to be named for another century, but a fact then as it is now.

Geneva hated the coast, feared the sea and the sudden storms that churned the water and drove bitter cold fogs inland. She despised San Francisco, called it Satan's playground. There were more babies and now Hilliard started construction on the house. It was built on land high over the city, above the fogs presumably, on the slope of what has since been named Russian Hill.

It took a year to build the house. Philippine mahogany, Belgian crystal chandeliers, chestnut paneling in the dining room, the entire southern exposure glass-enclosed with a wide Italian tile terrace outside. Hilliard was living his most treasured dream and loved it all. He was here, there, everywhere bossing the laborers, giving a hand with the stonework of the fireplace in the master bedroom, supervising the building of a wine cellar, consulting with suppliers. . . .

And Geneva kept on having babies. William, my father, was her last, the eleventh, and she never hated San Francisco less than on the day she wrote to her mother: "The Ground is never still and the Air is full of Clouds day and night with a Perpetual Rain that is either falling, has fallen or will Fall within the next few minutes. Sometimes the Rain hangs in the Air for days before it touches the ground. Chinamen Heatherns swarm in Town until I am too fearful of Them to venture outside these Walls that are like a Prison. . . ."

I found the letter in my father's papers. Perhaps he was sent to post it and forgot.

Poor Geneva, a prisoner in her mansion, forever a stranger in this land, forever yearning for the serenity of the Kansas fields, the sun glare in an endless sky, the austerity of the wooden church and pews, the comfort of her religion, which seemed so elusive in San Francisco, the devil's playground.

Hilliard built a box-house in 1868 and stayed there most of the time afterward, as far as I could tell from my father's narrative, doled out in crumbs over the years. A box-house, or French theater, was more than Geneva's Southern Baptist training could tolerate. There was music and dancing downstairs, a bar, tables for gambling, even a stage for entertainment. But its main attraction was upstairs where there were intimate dining rooms, each one large enough for only two, furnished with red velvet hangings, white linens, fine silver and crystal, and a divan.

In the sixties there were troubles in the mining country of Montana. Fire storms swept thousands of acres of parched forests in a continuing drought several years in a row. Water vanished. There was a depression in the early seventies and the price of copper plummeted. There were strikes and strike breakers and scabs and they fought with one another, and all of them fought against the ranchers who wanted and needed the scarce water that was being dissipated and polluted, and then there was an earthquake. It wasn't a major quake and no lives were lost, but several mines were buried under avalanches of rock.

The big mining companies held out during the depression, using the time to modernize their equipment, to bring mechanization to their mines. When there were demands for copper, they undersold the independents consistently. Finally, after half a dozen trips to his own holdings, and lengthy negotiations, Hilliard was forced to sell. A year later he was shot to death either inside his own box-house or outside it on the street. William, my father, was ten.

Geneva wasted not a moment. As soon as Hilliard was in the ground she began selling. Everything portable was carried away, everything permanent was sold where it stood. There were more debts than anyone had realized; her fortune was not great, but it was enough to move herself and her family back to her beloved Kansas. And she planned to do that as soon as the legalities permitted. She had no doubt that Hilliard's murder was God's just punishment.

I've often wondered about those hard-core fundamentalists, spending years of their lives on unadorned, uncushioned wooden benches. I wonder if after so many generations the babies aren't born with calloused bottoms. Perhaps they are and no one ever mentions it to outsiders, but they have the perfect means of identifying their own. I could imagine them approaching the Pearly Gates, the men dropping their trousers, women lifting their skirts, exposing their buttocks for admittance. . . . I never dared tell my father this fantasy. He spoke mildly of his mother and her yearning for home, and it was his audience, his children, who burned with hatred and resentment of her.

My father used to tell us the next part of the story almost as a ritual. You have to visualize the house to understand it, though. The house is three stories, with a basement and an attic. There is the entrance foyer, with a marble floor, and in his youth tubs of plants all about, some palm trees even. To the right is the formal drawing room, about thirty-five feet square, with a massive fireplace, and a curved staircase winding upward out of sight. There were two chandeliers in this room, parquet floors, Persian rugs, the walls covered with tapestries, stained glass panels outlining the windows, and so on. A Victorian monstrosity. It was like that throughout the house. Room after room, each done differently, with paneling, chandeliers, fireplaces, French windows, window seats curving under bay windows, a sun room jammed with tropical plants, exotics, whatever was costly and rare.

On the second floor there are six bedrooms and a large playroom where the children had classes with a private tutor. My grandmother refused to send them to school outside the house for fear the Chinamen Heatherns would kidnap them and sacrifice them on bloody altars.

The third floor has six more bedrooms, but they are smaller and less ornate, and four of them were used by servants. The attic is long, narrow, very dark; it housed a colony of bats. Or so my grandmother told the children, perhaps to keep them out of it.

There are two sets of stairs, the curved, wide steps leading up from the drawing room and another, narrower staircase in the rear of the house. The building is a children's heaven of hiding places, for games, of private nooks for quiet moments.

My father was ten, his brother David eleven, when the attorney first started showing prospective buyers through the house. The two boys, never far from each other, crept through the house miserably, hiding behind posts, behind tubs of palm trees, under staircases, listening, trying to force the buyers away with great efforts of will. They skulked about, always out of sight, always listening, prying, watching, and hating everyone who came to look.

They made plans to remain in the house when it was sold, to live in it forever, always out of sight, sneaking out at night to forage, never suspected. . . . A Mr. and Mrs. Wyckoff returned several times and brought a decorator with them, and mentioned to the attorney that finally they had found a house large enough for their eight children.

William and David knew their plan was doomed. There was no way they could hide from that many children, any more than a stranger could have hidden from them.

"We went to the cellar where we had our bundles hidden and sat down and looked at the stuff and at each other and I guess we were both crying. I know David was. I kept thinking there had to be a way. Our father had told us where there was gold, and we believed him, and knew that if we ever got back to that Kansas farm we'd never leave it again. Mother would buy a farm and put us to work on it from sunup to dark every day but Sunday, and on Sunday we'd sit in church all day. We knew all that." My father would pause then and look through time, seeing that boy and his brother just as I had looked back to see myself dancing at the edge of the lava. I wonder if he reached back and reassured the boy that it would work, if that reassurance had been felt somehow, had given the boy the courage he had needed to go through with the next plan they devised.

"I said to David, 'I just ain't going.' And he looked at me with his mouth opening and I knew he had meant to say exactly the same words to me. And in that second we decided. We were not going to be dragged back to a corn

field in Kansas. We would hide and after she was gone
with the others we'd work and save our money and when
we had enough we'd go find that gold our father had told
us about."

"But how did you live?" one of us always asked, usually
Wanda or I. Randolf seldom asked anything or com-
mented; he sat unmoving and watched the story unfold
as if in a trance. I have always felt sorry for Randolf;
he should have run away from home to prospect for gold
when he was young. I see that same hungry yearning
searching look sometimes when he is preoccupied staring
out a window at nothing at all. No one should go through
life with that hunger gnawing away inside.

But Father would not be hurried, or be cajoled
into telling his story out of sequence. "The house was
like a crazy asylum those days, my mother and the older
children running around packing, sorting through stuff,
servants packing, hauling, carrying, nailing up crates,
and us younger children being chased out of one room after another, ordered out to play, or to run fetch this or
that. Some of the girls kept on crying all the time. They
were afraid of Indians in Kansas: they knew what had
happened to their grandparents and aunts. Some of the
older boys were talking about getting guns and going Indian hunting, and about the horses they would breed and
make a million dollars a year. And Mother was everywhere at once. You'd think a woman who'd had eleven
children would have been tireder than she was, but she
managed to boss every bit of the packing, the sorting,
stacking of crates into separate areas—stuff to be shipped
on ahead, stuff to be taken, stuff being sold, given away.
She was a woman of iron. David and I used to whisper
ourselves to sleep at night, and we mostly talked about
what she would do to us when she found us." He paused
and thought, then said, "We were planning to hide out,
but we didn't expect to get away with it. That's how it
was. We were going to make the effort as if we expected
success when all the time we were worried about what
she'd do to us when she found us again."

The night before the move, the boys crept from the house
into the woods that were thick then on Russian Hill. There
were groves of iron oak and pine, with places that had no
understory growth at all, having been grazed clean by the
herds of goats that ranged on the steep slopes, but with

other places as dense as any African jungle with tangled briars and creeping vines. They had made a "cave," concealed it with boards covered with brambles, and inside it they waited for the next four days. Two times they heard the voices of the searchers come near, then recede.

My father was reticent about the next few weeks. They stole food, eggs from the small farms on the hill, vegetables and fruit from the gardens, whatever they could find. The search on the hillsides was abandoned and resumed in Chinatown. Geneva had become convinced that the Chinamen Heatherns had abducted the boys, that they were either on their way to China already for the private foul amusements of a greasy warlord, or else were being hidden in a swampy, rat-harboring basement, waiting for the right vessel to dock that would then take them to their unspeakable fates.

Later, when they slipped into town to take up life in the streets, the boys found posters offering a reward of five hundred dollars for information leading to their safe return to their mother's bosom. No one informed on them. No one even noticed them. It was not uncommon for boys of ten or eleven to be out working. For a time they toyed with the idea of having one of them turn in the other, collect the reward, and then escape once more, but this time with a stake. Their talk now was simple bravado; they were frightened and cold and hungry most of the time; by accomplishing what they had said they would do, they seemed to have destined themselves to early deaths from exposure or starvation. They talked even less persuasively of giving themselves up, of voluntarily returning to their family, to the corn farm in Kansas, taking up the plow, etc., etc.

Perversely, they began to feel that their mother had abandoned them, that she had welcomed the opportunity to leave them behind. If she hated them so much that she left them in the cold, foggy city without money, food, or clothes, then she would never allow them to return. Gradually the talk of going home faded from their conversations.

They stole when they could, they sneaked into empty buildings and slept when they could, and finally David got a job on the wharf, cleaning a fishing boat. Now they had food and a small but reliable income, and eventually

William also was hired by the boat captain and for the next few years they made out.

"Tell us about the gold," Randolf would say, tired of the tribulations.

Father nodded. He was almost ready to tell about the gold. But first, just a little bit more about San Francisco and the life they led. "We stayed on the docks most of the time, working, running errands, listening, watching, fighting, doing what boys have been doing since the beginning of time. San Francisco was booming again after the depression, buildings going up everywhere, the bay getting filled with garbage to make even more land. Nob Hill and Telegraph Hill were getting crowded with mansions, each one grander than the last. The railroads were being built all over the coast and the railroaders were back and forth spending their payrolls; miners with new gold to spend; schools getting built; streets put in; it was alive like it's never been since. A miner would come in with a new strike and the next day you'd have thought a plague had struck and the population had been scared away, the way they trekked out. There were ships from all over the world, bringing in immigrants—Chinese, Japanese, Russians, Irish, German. . . . And that was before the big flood of Russians who were refugees from the war with Japan. David and I never went to school much those days"—he didn't fool us, we knew he hadn't gone at all again until he was grown—"but we picked up stuff—enough Spanish to get by, a smattering of Russian, a bit of Chinese and French. And we read a lot, whatever we got our hands on. We saved some money so that we could buy a kit and head for the hills."

Randolf would shift nervously and lean forward now. He didn't care about early San Francisco. He wanted to hear about living in the wild hills and finding gold.

"We had a mule, tools and a Civil War musket, food and the clothes we wore. David was sixteen, I was fifteen, and we headed east by northeast. Our father had spoken of the most likely places that he intended to get back to one day, places he said he knew had gold just like he knew the sun would come up. There had been a strike in Alaska and the real gold-fever victims had headed up that way by then, but we weren't quite ready for that, and besides, we knew where there was gold. We never doubted a minute that our father knew what he was talking about.

It never occurred to us that if he had been that certain he might have gone up to Rogue River and dug up the fortune himself."

He told about the hardships of the long trip up the California valley, through the redwood and Douglas fir forests, where they skirted logging camps, having heard many rumors of the loggers that were frightening enough to make young boys more wary of them than of the Indians who still made sporadic raids through the area. They lived on game as much as possible, hoarding their beans and salt pork in anticipation of the long cold wet winter they knew lay ahead of them.

Sometimes, thinking of those two boys, hardly more than children, surviving in the wilderness for sixteen months as they did, I wonder if my own son, Scotty, could have lived through their ordeal, and I decided he couldn't have. A year and a half without vitamins, penicillin, allergy treatments, shelter. . . . He would have died. He broke out in hives on a two-week camping trip and had to be hospitalized.

They found gold, almost exactly where their father had said it would be. It wasn't a large strike, not a bonanza to flood the area with miners, but it made them both wealthy enough for my father to decide to head East and go to school, and for David, who was eighteen, to equip himself for a trip to Alaska and the even richer fields there.

My father went to school, then to the Columbia University School of Mines and came out a geologist. He went to Germany and studied some more, then on to France, England, and Italy, back to the States, where he met and married my mother and took her home to San Francisco. He bought back the house with the rest of his fortune. Two years later the big earthquake struck and the next day I was born. My mother hated San Francisco from then on.

I had a phone call from Scotty a week or so ago. He was calling from Ponta Delgada in the Azores.

"Mother, it's fantastic! In some places it looks like toothpaste was squeezed out of a tube and fell over. In other places you can see ooze lines where lava started up, then the process stopped and there is just this long line of basalt bubbles. Lava hangs from some of the upthrusts like oversized grapes. It flowed and made formations exactly like travertine curtains in caves. . . ."

Scotty is a geologist. I wonder if there is a gene that causes geology to erupt in the bloodstream. He is with a team studying the mid-Atlantic rift nearly two miles under the Atlantic Ocean. I can't bear to think of him in that tiny ocean craft, sinking, sinking. . . . Of course, he assures me often that the *Alvin* is the safest submersible ever built, and I think but never say, like the *Titanic*.

The excitement in his voice caused me to smile and think fleetingly of that small girl who danced at the sight of a lava field. "This is creation itself, Mother! Material coming up from the depths of the earth to create new lands!"

My father had been just as excited when he read an article about the discovery of mountains under the Atlantic Ocean. "It's Atlantis!" he had said. "Plato was right all the time. The land was submerged by a catastrophic earthquake, and one day, in your lifetime, man will find a way to get down there and explore those mountains just like they're exploring mountains on the surface of the earth, uncovering gold, silver, diamonds. Down there they'll find the ruins of a civilization so advanced they'll make us look like primitives!"

My son: "It's creation, Mother! Land is being created now, at this time, spreading the ocean floor, widening it, taking the North American continent farther from Africa to accommodate the land that is being formed."

And once, scornfully, impatiently, he had said of my father, "Oh, they did the best they could, but they simply didn't have the technology, the methods of forcing the secrets out into the open the way we have now."

Before my father's time they believed the seas were shallow basins of more or less uniform depth that filled with deposits, wind- and rain-driven particles that accumulated in time to cause new lands to rise to start the whole cycle over again.

And at a time men believed that chief Llao and chief Skell threw thunderbolts at each other and burned the mountains.

Facts. Data. More facts. I lie in this bed, with something pressing me down, and wonder if there will be aftershocks, if they will be even more severe than the original earthquake, and if I'll survive this night. This seems the only truth I know: that I cannot move, that it is very dark, and outside the sea sounds close and loud. Now I should rest, sleep if possible. I am much too old to stay awake all night worrying about my father, dead since 1932, worrying about my son, who wants to dance two miles down in the ocean.

3

I dozed and Louis kept getting between me and real sleep. His today-face was superimposed on, and gradually replaced, his twenty-six-year-old face, which in turn yielded, like a view through a kaleidoscope that looks into time through magic mirrors.

He keeps trying to reenter my life. Last week when I dismissed the taxi at the foot of our hill, the driver protested. "Lady, that's a steep climb and it's pretty late. You sure you want to walk?"

"Yes, quite sure." I took money from my purse, put the purse inside the suitcase and locked it again. "Just deliver this to Miss Holstead. I do this all the time, and she'll understand."

He took the fare and tip, looked dubious for another moment, shrugged and drove off, and I started to walk through the cool mist. Jackie Wonder, I kept thinking. Jackie Wonder. He would solicit good fiction from good writers and hide their stories in single columns between shots of pubic hair and rouged nipples. The nonfiction would be how-to sex articles alternating with learned and elegant articles about the state of the nation, or the world, included to satisfy the social conscience. There would be expensive full-page ads for gin, vodka, vermouth, whatever, all crammed with subliminal messages: fuck, screw, sex, drink, buy! Actually the sex might be played down, have a secondary role, with violence taking top dollar. Violence outsells sex, that's the latest word, and violent sex sells best of all.

We had always used advertising solely to support the fiction, poetry, the art, and now the magazine would be used to prop up the advertising. It was like watching a beloved child become a whore, or worse, a pimp. I couldn't bear to dwell on it.

Mr. Mirov's house, I remembered, passing a high-rise where Mr. Mirov's house used to stand. Mirov wasn't the name he left home with, but some immigration official hadn't been able to spell or pronounce that one, and on entering America he had become Mr. Mirov. My brother Randolf and I used to fly past his house in Randolf's wagon and he would come screaming out, trailed by wife, children, dog, cat, goats, shrieking at us that we were going to be killed. His English was very good; his wife never learned to speak it at all, and the children spoke a mixed language that was neither one nor the other. Sonya was my best friend for many years.

Kresge's house, still there, decrepit, but I remember when it was built. We were chased from the site time after time by a cursing foreman who taught us many new words. Now the steps, fifteen of them, that permit one to ascend without making the wide-swinging detour. This was where Louis and I stalled, before the detour was put in; he had tried to go straight up the hill. We had been married for three months, the automobile was a birthday gift from his parents, and he was not a good driver. The car stalled, slid backward again and again when he tried to shift into low gear to climb the hill. I clung to the door, petrified, afraid to move, as if any motion would accelerate the downward slide and send us crashing into Mr. Mirov's house below. In that way, stalling, sliding, jerking erratically from side to side on the narrow street, we made our way back down the hill to stop finally at the Mirov house. And Mr. Mirov came out, followed by wife, children, dog, etc.

I thought Louis would cry as he sat staring ahead, his face so rigid that any break at all would dissolve it entirely. I didn't speak. I had already told him the way my father drove up the hill in his Ford, but this was a new Chrysler and didn't need special treatment, didn't need smoothed-out hills or wide curves. We circled the hill for the next half hour, looking for a more likely street on which to ascend, and in the end we took the same route my father always used.

I smiled as I climbed the stairs. Poor Louis, so sulky for the next hour, daring me to mention to my parents the trouble we had had getting there.

. The fog was thinner as I climbed the hill and I was sorry. Now I could see the sharp edges of the condominiums that blotted out the sky and substituted pale orange lights every ten feet for starlight. A high fence hid the grounds, and a guard in a lighted cage didn't even glance up as I passed. Perhaps I would live in something like that, I thought, averting my head, refusing to see it. Across the street was the Farr house, now apartments, well kept up, better maintained than my house. I could do that, I thought. God knew I had enough room.

A new cloud of fog descended and I was grateful and could walk alone and watch for the Farr children, who waited in hiding for Randolf and leaped out at him when he passed by. At least three times a week he had a fight with one of the Farr boys, sometimes more than one. They rolled around in the dirt and no one ever got hurt. I think he would have missed it if the Farrs had moved away before we were all grown. I heard a trolley off to my right; it could have been almost anytime in my entire life, walking up the hill in the fog with the comforting sound of the trolley muffled in the distance.

We used to have a yard between the house and the street, but they widened the street, put in sidewalks, sewers, underground wires, I don't know what all, and with each improvement my yard was sliced away a bit more. Now the house is only ten feet from the sidewalk. There was light on each of the three floors that night and while it was cheering to think of the busy people inside, I didn't want to see any of them, or have to explain why I had come back so soon, or think of the electric bill, or anything else. I wished there was a way I could get in and have coffee and get to my room without seeing even Dorrie, but I knew that was impossible.

She must have been waiting for me; when I approached she opened one of the double doors and let me in. No one else was in the foyer. I could hear voices from the living room to the right, although the doors were closed, and voices of the television to my left.

"You sick?" Dorrie asked, examining me closely as she helped me with my coat, which was wet by then. I realized my hair was wet, and suddenly the chill that had been accumulating seized me. I shook my head. "Come on, let's get something hot, and a drink." She led and I followed, through the wide hallway to the kitchen, which was empty. "I shooed everyone out," she said, as if reading my thoughts. "Told them I was going to wax and would kill anyone who set foot in here tonight."

They would have believed her on both counts. She could take a notion to wax a floor at midnight and she was capable of killing anyone who bothered her too much. Dorrie is five feet eight or nine and weighs about a hundred eighty pounds and is not at all fat.

"Have you eaten?"

I told her yes without remembering if I had or not.

She nodded. "Why don't you go on up to your room and I'll bring you a sandwich and coffee and a drink. You're soaked. Crazy idea, walking home on a night like this. Crazy."

I was halfway up the stairs when she caught up with me. "Almost forgot something," she muttered, and stayed by my side when I opened the bedroom door, where I stopped and gasped. The room was filled with red and white carnations. On the vanity, the chest of drawers, both the nightstands, the end table by the chaise, every flat surface had a vase of red and white carnations.

"My God! Who died?"

"Nobody died. It's that crazy Louie. Had a truck deliver them today, insisted they all be put in your room up here." She looked about in disgust, and turned to leave.

"He's senile," I said. "Call someone to come take them away."

"Senile, crazy. I don't know. He needs a keeper, that's for sure. He was here yesterday and again today and said he'll be back tomorrow. He knows we're planning a party."

"He can't come!"

"Sure. I know. You want them out now, tonight?"

"My God, this looks like a funeral parlor."

We put the flowers in the hall outside my room and I

closed the door and leaned against it, weak with fury at Louis, crazy Louie, senile Louis.

We met, married, divorced, all within a year. That was crazy, I thought, undressing slowly, feeling stiff and tired, and very depressed. It was too much to have to deal with cra—Louis now. Why didn't he just go away, drop dead, start dancing naked in public and get put away. He, thank God, was not my problem, except sporadically, but Dorrie was.

What would I do about Dorrie? Where would she go? I sat in front of the fire and rubbed my eyes and tried not to think about Dorrie and the house and crazy Louie and red and white carnations.

But Louis won't go away. Even now, trapped here, waiting for help, or the rising tide, whichever comes first, Louis insists on intruding, on forcing his way before my inner eye, both as he is now and as he was when I fell in love with him. How different it would have been if his mother had died while he was away in school. We would have remained together, had children. I would be rich now.

I was still in college, and he had his first job with Hutton, Wainwright, and Carmichael when we met, and I didn't even realize he was the son of the Carmichael of the title. If I had realized, it would have meant nothing to me. He was a working man in an office, that was enough to know. Louis was shy and gentle and not very large, very like my father actually. I graduated and signed a contract to teach elementary school the following year and he asked me to marry him the same week. That summer when I went home, I met his family. I should have known then, but I didn't. His mother wanted us to wait a year, for my contract to be fulfilled, for Louis to spend some time abroad meeting the right people, for him to gain business knowledge and experience, for me to mature, for it all to fall apart.

We eloped instead.

The pressure started almost immediately. His mother moved to New York, where she took an apartment on Fifth Avenue in order to acquaint herself with the Eastern branch of the company, she said, but in truth to wreck our marriage before there was a child. Poor Louis never had a chance, and I was too young and ignorant and happy to know what to do about it, even to know there was a situation I should do something about.

Last week when Louis came to see me I tried to imagine what life would have been like if we had had a child that year, and failed. I couldn't imagine it at all.

"Did you get my flowers?" he asked, glancing about as if searching for them. We were downstairs in the television room.

"I got them and sent them all over to Women's Hospital. I'm sure the patients there appreciate them."

"Don't be hard, Emily. Don't be hard with me."

"What do you want, Louis?"

He is seventy-four, a frail, little, crazy rich man. His hair is white now, his face looks scarred it is so lined and wrinkled; he is nicely tanned from many months in the sun each year, down at Palm Springs, or in Jamaica, or somewhere. He wears heavy glasses and there is a hesitation in his walk, as if his feet are uncertain of each step. And he is shrinking. That is sad, that he is shrinking. His head is starting to look oversized, like a precocious child's head. His body is like an adolescent's.

"Emily, come to lunch with me, please. I want to talk with you."

"We can talk right here. If you're hungry I'll get you something."

"I'm not hungry," he said petulantly, that same old tone. "I just want to talk without a dozen people tramping through."

"Louis, I'm very busy. I don't have time to go out to lunch, and I don't have time for a long conversation with you, so just tell me what it is you want."

"Emily, what happened with us? It was so good. . . ."

"Oh, God, not now, not again," I said, eyeing the door.

"Just tell me if it was true, what she said."

"It was a lie. You know it, and you've always known it. A jealous little boy wrote a vicious letter to the principal. The principal had been tipped to report anything of interest concerning me to your mother without delay. He delivered the letter to her and she had me fired."

"She wouldn't have lied about something like that?" Louis said, but over the years a question mark had started to punctuate the sentence, and it had become a plea for reassurance.

"She lied, Louis. You know all this. Why are you here now bringing up all this again?"

"I have to know," he said, almost in a whisper. "I have to know everything. She made me get the divorce. You know that, don't you? She said you were having an affair and she had proof of it. Our attorneys said she had proof. What should I have done, Emily?"

"You should have believed me because you knew she was lying and I wasn't. I have to get back to work, Louis."

"Wait a minute. Emily, the boy, he's mine, isn't he? Scott is my son, isn't he?"

That jolted me; I sat down hard on the sofa. "Your son? He was born in 1940, Louis. In England. We were divorced in 1928. What are you talking about?"

"I saw you in England."

"We had tea!"

"But he is mine, isn't he, Emily? Scott is, isn't he?"

"Louis, please go now. Just go away and don't come back. I'm tired and busy and I don't have time for your nonsense!"

Louis came to sit on the sofa by me. He tried to take my hand. I jerked away and moved to a side chair. "I figured it out," he said, "the time, dates, everything. I know. I know."

He looked at me with a crafty expression, a little brown gnome with tendons and veins that seemed to be trying to force their way out through his hands and neck, and the refrain kept going through my head, *Crazy Louie, Crazy Louie.*

"Emily, you're having a party, aren't you? To announce your engagement?"

Crazy Louie, Crazy Louie.

"Are you going to marry Kodel?"

"I'm going back to work," I said, and started for the door.

"You can't do it, Emily. You're still my wife, you know. You still have my name, our son has my name, you can't marry someone else. I won't let you."

"You're talking like a madman. You got married again!"

"That doesn't count," he said. "It wasn't like what we had. It was a convenience, that's all. A convenience. Remember how we used to play, Emily? Remember how it was when we were together? Remember?"

I remembered, but the memory was bracketed by accusations and dismissal from school and the threats of her attorneys, the scandal of a divorce in 1928, my mother's reactions. . . .

"I want you back, Emily. My God, I'm an old man and I've wanted you for fifty years! You made me feel strong and tall and no one else has ever done that! I was a man with you, wasn't I, Emily? I was a man!"

He was looking past me, watching himself in that other time, watching us together. Tears were in his eyes. "You made me feel tall and strong," he said again.

"It's been almost fifty years! We've made our lives apart, Louis! That was another lifetime entirely. It has nothing to do with us anymore." He was weeping. I just wanted to hit him, to slap him to his senses. "Louis, get yourself a young woman, a young vigorous woman who wants to go with you on a world cruise or something. You'd feel young again."

He shook his head, oblivious of the tears. "I've tried young women. They don't make me feel like you did."

I knew: strong and tall. "Then for God's sake get some elevator shoes and wear padded suits, but get out of here! Get out and leave me alone!"

I was cruel. I could have been kinder to him, tried to reason with him, but I was impatient with his tears, his whining voice, his insane declaration of fatherhood. I did the best I could. He followed me into the foyer. "If you didn't care, why did you keep my name?"

"If your name was Emily Krump, you'd keep Carmichael too!"

I wept a little because I too had looked back and watched those two happy children playing with each other. He *had* been tall and strong then, at least when we were together. Did he shrink every time he left our apartment, or only in the presence of his mother, who forced him again and again into the little-boy role? If only she had died while he was in school, I thought again, and then I called Maury, because even if Louis was pitiable and crazy, he was an influential, wealthy man; he knew many people and could hire others to do whatever dirty work his insane mind decided upon. Once he tried to get the colonel to fire me, and another time he had tried to buy the mortgage on my house, presumably in both instances to establish some kind of dependency role upon me. His mother's true son. Maury's answering service took the call.

"Aunt Emily? Are you all right?" It was Karen, my great-niece. She opened the door enough to stick her head in. She looked anxious. No one had expected me home from New York so soon. Such a life as we live, I thought, keeps complacency at bay.

"Come in, come in. Where's Katherine?"

"Oh, she's around somewhere. Do you have a minute?"

I nodded and sat down on the couch before the fire-place, patted the cushion beside me and waited. They wanted something. If it was just chatter, they came to-gether; if they wanted something, Karen was the one who broached it. Now she looked at the fire miserably and didn't speak until I coughed.

"I'm sorry," she said then. "It's hard. You know Mother and Dad separated last fall. . . ."

Karen and Katharine are almost seventeen, twins, one tall, fair, and lovely, the other short, medium-dark, and lovely. Karen was the short one. She looked like my sister Wanda at her age, which is probably why she is the spokesman for them when they want something from me.

"Karen, I give you three minutes, okay? Mr. Farber is coming on business and I have to have some notes ready."

"Something *is* wrong, isn't it?" she cried, and jumped up. "I don't want anything, it's nothing. I'm sorry I bothered you now."

"Sit down, you nit, and speak up. No preliminaries. I know your mother and father and your grandmother and grandfather and more other relatives than you've even dreamed of. What do you want?"

She looked at her watch and took a deep breath. "It's Mother and Dad. They both want us, or they want to split us up and each have one, or take turns, you know, here six months, there six months, and so on. They do love us, you know, they just don't love each other, and we love them both, but we don't want to live with them, not like that. Aunt Emily, can we stay here with you?"

They were with me, but temporarily; that had been stressed in December, when they had first come to visit.

"We'll work for you, help Dorrie, do your filing, what-ever you want us to do." Filing was my one constant bitch. No one else could do it in a way that let me find anything, and I hated doing it myself. "We'll get part-time jobs and pay room and board, anything."

I don't know what my face revealed, but she dimpled, then said in a dead serious tone, "We'll even intercept craz—Mr. Carmichael and not let him in to bother you."

"Out! Beat it! Three minutes are up. I'll speak to Judith and Laurence. No promises. I'm not even sure I want two pesty girls hanging about."

She jumped up, leaned over and kissed me on both cheeks, and ran from the room. Katherine was probably waiting in the hall. When she was gone, I paced and called myself coward over and over until the word lost all meaning. I am a coward, always have been. But that was a low point. I couldn't tell her there would be no house for her to stay in, that I would have to give it up, move into an apartment—maybe government housing. Or I could become a bag lady, live out of a shopping bag, sleep in flower boxes here and there, scrounge in garbage cans. . . . They would write stories about me for Sunday supplements, or a *New Yorker* profile would detail my rise and fall, as if I had been an empire unto myself, or my nephews and nieces and the young writers and artists I had encouraged would collect nickels and dimes, put on a charity benefit for me, have a presentation dinner that cost more than the gift, and then, having done their duty to the past, walk merrily into the future feeling virtuous and generous.

Maury would scold and point out how well off I would be now if I had followed his advice over the years, how to assure a golden retirement one must plan and save and invest and watch the pennies. . . . He would be right, but that didn't mean I wanted to hear it. Tony would ask me to marry him again, so he could take care of me. And he would be right, but that too I didn't want to hear.

"Emily?"

I whirled to see Maury entering. "Don't lecture—" He looked awful, his clothes rumpled, his face ashen, his eyes red-rimmed. "What happened?"

"Estelle had a stroke two nights ago," he said, collapsing onto the couch. "I just stopped by to tell you on my way home. I had to talk to you."

I locked the door, sat by him, and held him close while he wept on my breast.

4

Our apartment was very small, two rooms and a bath. Everything was yellow and white and Dresden blue, and the afternoon sun brightened the rooms. I still had long hair. My father had begged me not to cut it, and then Louis had, and I wore long dresses because the school authorities insisted upon that. I can see myself now in that sunny living room, dressed in a long white dress with a blue sash, dressed like a little girl on her way to a party. No makeup, God forbid!

Perhaps there was a time, when I was three or four, or even younger, when I was cute, but not since then. I was never pretty, not even handsome, and I never had enough patience to work at looking smart. My hair was straight, thick, and too pale to be brown, too dark to be blond. My nose has been my special curse, too long and narrow, like a female Holmes impersonator. I was flat-chested so long that we all gave up hope of my ever developing a womanly form—my form never changed, but hope died. This time of my life when I am seventy (almost) I find that my figure is fashionable, and there was a brief period in the late twenties when I didn't feel self-conscious. I guess big boobs will come back in style soon and for another fifty years girls and women will look at illustrations with hatred and envy, take vitamins, do special exercises, buy special bras. . . . What is it for? Not the men who love them. No man ever said to me, "Hey, you'd be a good-looking woman if you just had bigger tits!"

If I could get to my notebook I would jot down: check cycles on changes in morality, promiscuity, tolerance, etc. Most of the articles I have suggested over the years have come from just such random thoughts. Some of the articles have been fine, have been followed up to book length eventually. I have a special shelf for those books and I feel as proud of them as if I had written them all myself, or my children had.

I was thinking of our first apartment and Maurice Farber. I opened the door to admit him that day; he was only a few years older than I, nervous-looking, hesitant, obviously a reluctant courier. "Mrs. Carmichael?" I nodded and he handed me his card self-consciously. I don't suppose he had had much occasion before that to present his card to people. He was one of *her* attorneys, a very junior member of the firm. His name was not on the letterhead yet.

Maurice Farber changed my life more than anyone else, more even than Louis did.

We sat opposite each other on straight chairs with a white painted table between us. There was a bowl of yellow and white chrysanthemums on the table; the petals were turning brown and falling off.

"Mr. Huchins sends his respects and wishes to inquire if you will be kind enough to see him at your convenience in his office."

I shook my head. I wished I had thrown out the flowers that morning. There is a time when one hour means the difference between beauty and death, and that hour had passed for them.

"Mrs. Carmichael, perhaps you don't understand. . . ."

"I understand all I need to. Everything they're saying about me is a lie! Everything!"

"Do you have an attorney to represent your interests, Mrs. Carmichael?"

I shook my head again.

"Mrs. Carmichael, do you understand the difference between an annulment and a divorce? If you will agree to the annulment, it will be as if neither of you had ever been married, there will be no blemish on your reputation, you simply go back to your maiden name and everything is as it was a year ago."

"In whose eyes, Mr. Farber? Not in mine. I know those nine months existed. Will an annulment restore my innocence?"

He blushed furiously and took a deep breath. "If there is a divorce, the grounds will be adultery, and you will have to live with that for the rest of your life, Mrs. Carmichael."

"I am not an adulteress! Louis knows I'm not!"

"Please, Mrs. Carmichael, permit me to recommend an attorney who will represent you, protect your interests in this matter. There is no need for you to see Mr. Huchins. Your attorney will handle everything for you."

I stood up. "I don't have any money, Mr. Farber. I could not pay an attorney."

He stayed for an hour, explaining about annulments, divorces, contingency fees, alimony, settlements. . . .

Finally I showed him out. "Tell your employer I am innocent. Whatever they think the evidence suggests to the contrary, it is a lie and Louis knows it is a lie. Ask him outright. He will tell you, he'd have to tell you. I don't want his money. I didn't even know there was any money coming to him until *she* talked about it. Louis knows that too. I won't take alimony, and I don't want a settlement. Would I allow myself to be branded a whore, taking money for living with my husband, then pretending it never happened?"

He left, but came back two days later. He was even more nervous than before. This time he avoided looking directly at me. I wondered if he had asked Louis.

"I have a paper for you to look over and consider, Mrs. Carmichael. It's a statement for annulment. In it you agree that you refused to have children, that's all."

"I won't sign it. It's a lie."

"It's a necessary lie, Mrs. Carmichael. Sometimes it is necessary to compromise, not to permit pride to bring about a catastrophe. No one wants to hurt you unnecessarily."

"What did Louis say?"

"He wouldn't talk about it."

"Does she keep him chained to her chair?"

"What do you . . . ?" He glared at me then. "You're hardly in a position to be sarcastic."

"What should I be then, Mr. Farber? Does she think I'll be shamed enough to creep into a closet and hide? Am I supposed to be grateful for her crumbs? Maybe a thank-you note is what she expects! She doesn't want this annulment to protect me! If she could have me drawn and quartered, she would. It's for Louis. There are still very respectable people who would never consider allowing their daughter to marry a divorced man. She must have had her eye on a girl for Louis for a long time, someone who is proper, who is wealthy, who is of a very good family, and poor Louis fell in love instead. What a shock that must have been, and she set out instantly to undo the damage, and now I won't cooperate. How much money has she put on the stick for you to hang out in front of me? How expensive is it to destroy a person's life?"

I caught him off guard. He would never make a good trial lawyer, I thought, and I was right—he has never taken a case to court. He looked guilty and then cross. "She is prepared to be more than generous," he said.

I laughed. "You're too young to be so pompous, Mr. Farber. Generous! Hah!"

"Mrs. Car . . . would it be possible for me to call you Emily? I think of her as Mrs. Carmichael."

I felt myself stiffen, more wary than before.

"You do well to be careful, Emily, but I'm not here to trap you. You're in a difficult position and you can't win, no matter how unjust all of this appears. The least damage will come to you through signing the papers for an annulment, accepting the settlement, which is truly generous, and making a new life for yourself. I am not your attorney, but since you refuse to consult one, I feel compelled to give you this professional advice, not biased by any factors, simply thinking of your welfare."

"I won't sign a lie."

"You are being stubborn, to your own detriment. For spite you will ruin the rest of your life, your reputation. You will be branded an adulteress in the eyes of the public."

"Mr. Farber, suppose I should consult an attorney. Could I win? Why is she so certain they can do this?"

He was embarrassed. "They have proof," he said after a

hesitation. "Mr. Huchins says the letter they have is suffi-
cient."

"Just the letter?" Who wrote it? A child!"

"I can't say. I didn't see it. Mr. Huchins has it in his
possession."

"A letter! Anyone can write a letter, say anything! You
accept that?"

"Mr. Huchins has no reason to lie about it, Emily. He
accepts it."

"So a phantom letter writer can destroy my life by ac-
cusing me of having a phantom lover." I went to the window and looked at the street below; children were playing
hopscotch, others were kicking a can up and down the
street. There was very little traffic. "I'll get a lawyer," I
said, not turning to look at Maurice Farber again. "I'll
fight adultery because it's a lie. My father has offered to
pay my legal expenses. You'd better tell them that." The
street blurred and I closed my eyes. "But for Louis to believe it, that's what is so hard to accept. Why didn't he
ever just ask me?" Maurice Farber made a throat-clearing
sound and I brushed my eyes with the back of my hand
and went back to the table. I would not weep before him.

"I'll report what you've said," Maury said, getting up. "I
think you are being wise, if I may say so."

When he came back he was gloomy. "It's the scandal,"
he said. "Mrs. Carmichael wants to know how much you
will accept for annulment."

"Hah! They know the phantom lover's a lie, and the
phantom witness a perjurer. They know they can't win!
That whole lie was meant to scare me."

He was red-faced when he said, "There is a counteroffer
I am to relate to you. If you will agree to move to Mrs.
Carmichael's apartment, live with her and your husband
there, no action whatever will be pressed."

I stared at him, bewildered and very alarmed at this
change. "You know I won't do that. She knows I won't.
She wanted us to live with her at the start and we refused."

Maury shuffled papers and looked at them intently. "If
you refuse, they will go ahead with the divorce
proceedings and charge you with desertion."

He had said it early, there was no way I could win. I
sat down hard and put my hand on his to stop the
senseless movements with the papers. "I could probably

fight that, too, couldn't I? There's no law that says a man and wife have to live with his family." I wasn't asking for advice and he understood that. "I don't care," I said then. "Let her do it. I just don't care."

Maury sighed deeply. He put the papers away. "What will you do, Emily?"

"I don't know. I can't teach again. Mr. Herscholtz made that very plain."

"Do you have train fare to go home?"

"I can't go home," I said sharply, warning him off that subject. My mother had been hysterical since I wrote to tell her what had happened. She blamed me, and would blame me no matter what she knew to be true. It was a scandal, a humiliation beyond bearing. If I went home she would want to hide me in the attic, with the colony of bats, and never let me out in public again.

Maurice Farber nodded. He knew all about such mothers, I learned later. He sat there, very straight and stiff and proper, never looking directly at me. He was thin, studious, tightly buttoned, with black hair that was too smooth, and a nervous mannerism of stretching his neck as if his collar chafed. He cleared his throat a lot, too. He had a New England accent, a Harvard education, and all the correct relatives and the correct fiancée. His life lay planned before him like a road map—at age twenty-eight turn here and go four years. . . . All so orderly, so easy. It was no wonder that he handled this grubby little affair with such distaste. How outside his sphere it must have seemed.

"Can you use a typewriter?"

"I can learn."

"I'll ask around. Perhaps I can come up with something that will do for you." He looked at me, averted his gaze, then shook his head. "Do you have money to live on until you find another position?"

"I have a paycheck coming, but I suppose they are holding it up on her orders, more pressure, that sort of thing."

"I'll find out," he said. "If it's due, you shall have it."

"Mr. Farber, aren't you working for the welfare of the wrong person, advising me, taking the trouble to find me a position, getting my check?"

He rose and went to the door, then gave me a long

puzzled look as if something he couldn't identify kept nagging at him. "I am," he said. "I know I am."

He found me a job, file clerk with an advertising agency, helped me move into a smaller, cheaper studio apartment, and when the divorce went through he brought me the papers and a bottle of champagne.

I had cut my hair for the occasion, and I was wearing a new short dress, and was very self-conscious of my knees and my naked neck. I was twenty-two, a divorcée, a flapper, and that night I got very drunk, another first, and slept with Maury Farber, who proposed the next morning.

"I want to marry you!" he said in wonder. "I want to get married!"

"You're engaged, Maury. It's been arranged for almost a year."

"But I love you! I loved you from that first day when you stood there in that ridiculous white dress and looked sixteen and I thought you were a wild woman."

"And now you know what you thought was right."

He shook his head, smiling at me, running his finger over my cheek. "I know you're the loveliest woman I've ever met and the bravest and the stubbornest, and the only one I want to marry."

I shook my head slowly. "I've been married, remember? I am married, no matter what those silly papers say."

"Do you still love him?"

"I don't know. I don't know now if I loved him or if it was excitement or what it was, but I can't marry again. Not now. Not yet." And Maury, what would it do to him to marry a woman in disgrace? I didn't ask. I knew. The firm would fire him. No respectable law firm would take him on. Another time, years later, I asked him, "Maury, why do we let them make laws to regulate our emotional lives? Marriage, divorce, adultery, what has this to do with the state, the welfare of the citizenry at large? Why can't we just be ourselves without fear?"

"You'd take the fun out of government," he said.

I shook my head with impatience. I was serious. "It's to control people, that's it. If they could find a way to control our breathing, they would. Everyone face east to breathe in the morning, west for the evening, north at night, the first offense a ten-dollar fine, then twenty-five, then imprisonment. If the people ever demanded freedom to breathe in an uncontrolled manner, chaos would result, anarchy would rule, it would be the end of civilization as we know it."

"You're a maniac."

"Probably. But I'm right for all that. And you know it."

And another time, even later, Maury exploded at me, "No, for God's sake, I won't lend you money to buy back that mausoleum! What do you intend to do with that hotel?"

"Live in it. Take Scotty home to grow up there where I grew up."

"It's a white elephant. The upkeep will kill you."

"I'll manage. But I need more money. It seems a woman can't get a mortgage loan."

"No. I'm sorry, Emily. For anything else in the world, but that. You know I've tried to give you money, jewelry, whatever I could over the years. You always refused, and now when you ask, I can't. Let me help you get a house in Connecticut, near the shore. You'd like it there, and I could visit you and Scotty. . . ."

"I have to go, Maury."

"Emily! Don't be a stiff-necked fool! That house will kill you. The next earthquake will crumble it like a house of cards and you know you can't get insurance to cover a fraction of it."

"Did I ask you for advice! Did you hear me ask you what I should do?"

"You never ask anyone for advice." His voice became heavy with sarcasm. "That's why you're trying to borrow money now."

"Don't get smartassed, Maury. It doesn't become you. I asked for a loan and you said no, that's that. I have to be going."

"Can I come to see you this weekend?"

"Of course. This has nothing to do with us."

But he didn't, or couldn't, understand that. He kept apologizing for weeks until I was bored with the subject. He kept explaining right up until the day I told him I was moving back to San Francisco, that I had money for the house, a job waiting, and movers hired.

"Who? Who let you have it?" he demanded, suspicious, furious, so certain until then that there was no way I could have managed it.

"It doesn't matter. It's done. You know the address, I

think. We're driving out, Dorrie, Scotty, and I, and plan to take a month for sightseeing along the way."

"Emily, please don't go. When will I be able to see you? I'm going to divorce Estelle. This is crazy. I want you, Emily, more than I ever did before. I want to marry you, to see you at breakfast, to look up and see you there, to know you're waiting for me, to feel you beside me during the night, take care of you when you feel rotten, bring you tea or ice cream. . . ."

"Maury, sh. Don't. You are the finest man I know, and I truly love you, but I won't marry you. Even if you were free, if you and Estelle hadn't married, I wouldn't. I can't explain it in any way that you'll understand, I know. But I would become your wife and no longer be myself. Can you see that? I would be waiting for you, my life revolving around you, my plans waiting for your plans to be made. I can't do it. I've been alone too long to become someone's wife, especially someone like you. You're an important man, doing important things, and no one should be allowed to hinder you. I would kill you, Maury. I know it because I know myself. I would demand too much, give too little."

We talked, then argued, then fought, then made love, and the next day I left for San Francisco. Maury has become important. He quit his job with the prestigious firm after two years, worked for the government through the early Roosevelt years, quit that, and wrote a book: *The Body of Law Versus—You!* That was the first. Later he worked as counsel for the Senate Judiciary Committee, and had to quit that also. He was a Harvard professor for over twenty years, and a volunteer ACLU attorney. He has written four books in all, each a beautifully reasoned, eloquent, brilliant analysis of our judiciary system, our federal, state, and local laws and how they are loaded against the public.

His last book, *The Perilous Century*, is dedicated to E. C. I can see a scholar, a thesis writer, poring over it, searching his references for the identity of E. C.

5

It is hard to tell if I am awake or asleep, a condition many people suffer throughout their lives, but relatively new to me. My dreams and my memories have been blurring at the edges, merging, forming something that is neither one nor the other. I have run several articles about dreams, dreaming, research into dreaming; I am something of an expert on the subject actually—because of extensive reading, not research as such. In fact, I am somewhat an expert on a great many subjects, assuming my writers do their homework and take care to present facts as they are known today, or believed, or acted upon as if they were believed. . . . Facts I have found to be nondurable, the result presumably of my having lived too long and having a rather good memory. It was a "fact" once that the many strata of materials found in the earth were caused by various minerals being dissolved in wide oceans and being deposited when the oceans dried up. My father gave me that example to prove that "facts" that are not accompanied by hard evidence are invalid, no matter how many of the pressing questions of the day they seem to satisfy.

"What's the matter, honey?" My father is sitting on the side of the bed, gazing at me sadly. "You're unhappy."

"Not unhappy, not exactly. Father, I don't understand anything anymore. Do you know what I mean?"

"We never understand things really. It's a game we play, honey, pretending we do, making things work, or pretending they work if they don't. It's just a game."

"You told me lies, and I trusted you. Everything you told me was wrong. You always went on and on about truth and I believed you. Truth based on facts, and that's a lie. I defended your lies."

He shakes his head, and he is no different from what he was when I danced in the woods that distant day. I even smell woodsmoke and the resin of pine trees. "Truth is taking into account all the known facts and summing them up in a general statement that does not refute, distort, ignore, or deny them. As new facts are discovered, or old ones invalidated, truth changes. There can be no absolute truth, no absolute reality."

"You gave me truth instead of faith and tradition. And the truth you gave is as variable as spring weather. Trying to keep and live by your truth is as futile as trying to wear a smoke ring. All you ever gave me was words! Sounds! Names of things we don't understand! And by making the right noise, saying a name, calling a number, we trick ourselves—you tricked me!—into believing . . ."

"Believing what, honey? What do you believe?"

"Nothing!"

But I used to believe in love and doing good and peace and grasping the world, using it to make everything better, understanding its secrets, the work scientists were doing. . . .

"Every stress you put on any system has to be relieved," he says, pontifically. "It might take years, or moments, but relief will be found. And the longer the period of stress, the more explosive the act of achieving relief."

I can't turn off my ears, can't cover them with my hands, and I believe my eyes are already closed. I say to him meanly, "For a million years or more the human race survived without knowing the truth of evolution, of cosmology, geology, the laws of harmonics. They survived, mated, wondered at the stars, tilled the soil, sang. They served many strange gods whose beginnings were always beneficent, but who inevitably became too destructive to tolerate and were cast out like Lucifer. Your god is being cast out now and everyone can see what a shallow god it was, how destructive it became."

He chuckles and I think he is fading, but I won't give him the satisfaction of looking to make certain. "Some people know what the truth is," he says, from a great distance. "They don't ask questions and they are happy. They *know*."

"They are stupid! What they know is nothing!"

"But they have peace." The words fade out to nothing, mingling with the surf.

Now that, I think, was a dream. Freud said we dream in order to preserve sleep, that sleep is necessary to purge the body of the wastes accumulated during the day. The sandman bags them in heavy-duty plastic and takes them away when he sprinkles sand on our eyes. Freud didn't say that part. Today they say we sleep in order to dream, that without dreams we go insane. You accumulate facts to arrive at a truth, and the truth is constructed out of dry sand with a high wind predicted. It is all a matter of time.

If I am not already dead, or if I don't die before the sun rises after this endless night, if I am able physically (I really don't know if I am seriously hurt or not; I have so little sensation from my body that I am suspicious), if this is not a dream that will fade when I awaken, then I shall pursue faith the first day that I am able to function.

It is pointless to pursue truth or facts or, through them, reality, and that leaves only faith as a goal. With each new set of facts that evolves a new truth, a new stress is put on reality, until eventually reality itself must shift, and we no longer can see the old reality.

With faith there is no such problem. There are no questions, no puzzling answers, no new shifts, no fault lines that must give to relieve disequilibrium. No psychic quakes. Faith imposes itself upon one, conditions one both in what to perceive and in how to perceive. Faith defines reality. It doesn't even matter what one has faith in, it is the act of having faith that sustains. "Why didn't you ever tell me that, Father?" I call out, but he is gone.

And faith is as far removed from facts and truth as milk is from moon cheese.

Around the world there are many seismological stations where automatic equipment measures seismic activity, which is earthquake activity. Computers are programmed to correlate computations and tell exactly where the earthquake occurred, measure its intensity, time its duration so quickly that the news is flashed out before the last rumble is quieted. So, why the hell aren't they here now digging me out?

There hasn't been any unusual aircraft activity, no helicopters scouting the damage. No governor or president assessing the millions of dollars of federal relief that will be needed to restore everything to its original precarious existence in an earthquake zone. There have been no sirens, no police trucks or fire trucks with loudspeakers telling the populace to remain calm. No looters have come yet, and that is the most discouraging datum of all. The center must have been well out at sea, and they think no land areas were affected, and likely no others were, just this one spit of headland, this one cliff where my house perched defiantly. Of course, it has only been a few minutes, but if they can put men on the moon, etc., etc. If you were not such a coward you would not be here, I remind myself.

I went to the office and broke the news and we all wept, Constance, Mike, Red, all of us. But I couldn't do the same thing at home, not yet. The twins are preparing their campaign to remain at my house; their cousin Warren is there using the darkroom in the basement, dogging Kenneth's every step; Homer is working on his novel; Kenneth, resting, conducting a seminar twice a week on photography, Regina Szacz and her eight-year-old son, who is a bed wetter. Where would they all go? They all have found something they need in my house, and when the time comes they will move on, and others will arrive to stay with me a week, a month, however long it takes to repair something that was damaged, or threatened, out in the real world.

Not now! Think of something far away. Think of London.

I was the overseas editor for *The Weekly News of the World,* now dead, gone, forgotten. The paper shortage during the war was fatal and the magazine died quietly and was never revived. I did little more than gather the stories as they came in from stringers, regulars, one-timers, and send them along each Wednesday to the New York office. When I applied for the job I was desperate enough that if they had said they wanted a woman who would belly dance in Soho, I would have taken it. Thursday and Friday were slow, things picked up a bit over the weekend, and by Monday and Tuesday everything was hectic up until noon Wednesday, when I cabled the New York office with what I had that was urgent, mailed the rest, and my week's work was over.

With the air raids going on there was a lot of news. London hadn't been hit yet, but shipping ports, airfields, aircraft factories—all had been heavily bombed during the past six weeks.

Paris had fallen and the Germans were bombing England, preparing to invade, everyone said. That seemed plausible. Do you want out? the home office kept asking, and I kept saying no, not yet. They thought it was bravery, dedication to duty, and it was simple desperation. I had to have my baby first. They didn't know I was pregnant much less due to deliver within days. Do you want out? Not yet. Good girl.

August, hot, clear days, bombing raids in the south, refugees. . . . Sorry, holidays are postponed on account of war. Intelligence reports indicated that an invasion was impossible because the Hun didn't have the landing equipment, hadn't trained the army in landing procedures. Other intelligence reports said they were gathering barges, sailing vessels, tug boats, everything that would float from all over Europe, and they were holding landing maneuvers. Or, they just wanted to stop the flow of materials from the ports, isolate Great Britain, take her out of the war as a supplier of materials. The items passed through my hands, on to New York, and I hardly was aware of them, could think only, What can I do now? I had picked out a small village on the southern coast near Bournemouth, where I had intended to go early in September to await the birth of my child, and the village had been bombed out of existence. Every day other coastal towns and cities and villages were bombed and I dared not leave London, and couldn't remain and bear my illegitimate child there.

September brought cooler, brisk weather. I walked to the office on Plumstead every morning; my time was nearly up. I would have to go into a hospital after all, have the necessary papers filled out, everything recorded. The sirens started to wail. A drill? Again? Then I heard the distant hum of planes and I knew, as everyone else on the streets knew, that this was no drill, not this time.

There are sound-associated memories that seem to be

unreal in the sense that there is little visual imagery, but
vivid audio details. I went to the Cape for one of the
moon shots, and what left a lasting impression on my
memory was the sound. First a roar, an earth-shaking,
bone-shaking blast that endured and endured, and finally
fading, left my body reverberating as if the sound was still
present, in another form. It was an experience for which
there are no words. Mind fuck is close, but it was more
than that; a soul fuck that left one stunned and somehow
changed.

London during the blitz was noise: the heavy drone of
bombers; the snarling, wailing screams of RAF fighters;
the staccato of the antiaircraft guns; the demonic howling
of the fire trucks and ambulances; the loudspeakers issuing
quiet, persistent instructions in perfect form; the yelping of
fire wardens, shelter wardens; the sounds of glass smashing
and walls exploding into rubble, beams crashing through
floors below; and then the relative quiet of the shelters
where voices were muted, and an occasional baby's cry
was louder than anything else there.

There is a visual memory. Incendiaries were dropped often, and usually did little damage because the organization
of the fire department was wondrous. One night I stood on
one side of the Thames and stared transfixed while a white
glare rose with blinding radiance just across the river from
me. It dazzled, and the river became a brilliant ribbon of
light all in an instant. The afterimage persisted for many
minutes. When the flares were yellow followed by puffs of
filthy smoke, they were oil bombs, and deadly. I never saw
one of them, and my memory of fire bombs is one of
unholy beauty and terror.

The sirens were inside my head, filling it, drowning out
the loudspeakers. I kept thinking, I should go home, I
should go home. And I did not know if I meant my apartment, or home New York, or San Francisco. I should go
home. I should go home. Someone shouted at me and I
hurried more, not to the shelter, past it, turned south, hurried, ran awkwardly, and thought, I should go home. I
should go home.

There were explosions and clouds of smoke and dust,
and no one was shouting at me any longer, but I ran,
thinking only of my own home, close by now. A bomb exploded in the sidestreet I was passing and I was thrown
down, heavily, and lay there for a moment catching my

breath, waiting to see if I would be killed. A hand hauled me up and a voice said, in wonder or fury, "Them bastards is bombing us!"

That was Dorrie Holstead.

I can't remember exactly how it happened that she moved in with me, but when Scotty was born three days later, she was there; the bombs were falling, and she delivered my son.

"He's lovely, Emily," she said. "Lovely."

I nodded. A distant explosion shook the walls, faded. "He was born in Bournemouth, June tenth, Dorrie."

Her eyes were like pale blue marbles, so round, so full of wonder. She was eighteen, or said she was eighteen. She could have been sixteen or twenty-three or -four. I didn't press it then or ever.

"No one will ever ask you, I'm sure, Dorrie, but if they do, will you tell them that?"

She nodded. "Sure I will, and who would know better than me, who was his nursemaid from the day he was born?" She took him from me and wrapped him closely in a flannel shirt. "Go on to sleep now, Emily. I guess we don't need a doctor after all, do we?"

Blackmail? Maybe it was. She went away and came back with a small paper suitcase that she had covered with flowered oilcloth. "Not very lovely, is it? But it keeps m'things dry. I got a friend works down at the registry office, and she said you should keep the babe's birth certificate copy in your kit. Not a very good copy, but better than none at all, seeing's how the original's been burned up and lost."

She produced a piece of flimsy gray paper with a stamp that looked official, and blanks to be filled in. "What you do," she said, surveying the form at arm's length, "is get some other papers and carbons and draw a line where it's to be signed, and write on the top copy, not too hard, you know, just so's something comes through. Who's to say it ain't legal then?"

I asked her once why she had so little accent. There were many people in England whom I couldn't understand at all. On a bus one time I had to ask for interpretation from a fellow passenger when the driver called out the stops, each more unintelligible than the last.

"Me and Molly Prentiss go to every movie that comes along," she said. "We practice the dialogue on each other until we get it down pat. I can do a perfect Myrna Loy. You want to hear?"

When I was ordered to return home, in December, it seemed natural that Dorrie should come with me. "Only till you make other arrangements," she said, "and I get a real job. Right?"

"Dorrie, look, I have no money, except what I earn. And that's damn little. I can't afford a full-time nurse-maid, housekeeper, whatever. I can't pay you."

"Now that's not to worry about, Emily. You'll have to hire someone to take care of Scotty, won't you? And who knows him better than me? And look at you! Your skirt's too loose and your jacket's too big for you, bags in the back right across the shoulders. You paid too much for it and it looks terrible on you. I can sew, make your clothes, and they'll fit you. Count on that, Emily, I wouldn't let you out in a suit like that, I wouldn't. So you just let me bed down with you and the little fellow and learn the ropes of New York, you know, and then off I go, like a bird. You have to have someone look after him while you're working, and your mum's not going to be good for anything like that, now is she?"

"But what about your family? Your parents?"

"Gone," she said solemnly. "Bombing raid down on Birmingham. There ain't nobody for me to stay about for." She lied about that, she admitted unabashedly years later when she went home to visit them.

"But they could be bringing me home to fire me, and then what? I won't have a job, no money, nothing. What will you do in a strange country?"

She laughed. Her teeth were absolutely beautiful, still are. She could model for toothpaste ads. "You won't starve, Emily. Not you. And not me either. Deal?"

When Scotty was grown he told me about his relationship with Dorrie. "You were soft," he said. "A lecture, maybe taking my allowance away for a while, that was enough, but Dorrie, wow! She believed in spankings. And she could spank like a wrestler. One time I spied on her and her gentleman friend." He grinned, then went on, "She caught me at it, and didn't say a word, but grabbed my arm and marched me to my room and locked the door. She pulled down the shades, all the time hanging on to me, and I was getting good and scared. After the room was secured, her word, she began to undress me, and I fought back. I was nine, maybe ten, and big and strong, but I was like a kitten in her hands. She got my pants down and turned me over her lap and laid it on me like the devil. Never a word. When she was done, she dumped me on the bed, marched out without a backward glance, and never mentioned it at all. I was afraid to meet her anywhere in the house for a week after that, but as far as she was concerned it was all over."

"Was it so bad, growing up with two mothers?"

"Not really. Her gentlemen friends liked to show off by doing things with me, teaching me stuff, like tying knots, how to make and set traps, stuff about the car engine, things like that."

If it hadn't been for Dorrie I never would have had the nerve to buy back the house. It never would have occurred to me that I could manage it.

One night, after the thought had occurred to me, I tried to talk Dorrie out of our lives for the last time. I had tried before, first about getting an education, training for a good job, anything. She had laughed at that. "What for? I hated school, got out of the dungeon soon's I learned to read and do figures. You think I'd go back to that? Not on your life! And I had me a job. Remember? No thanks. Not again."

When Scotty was two, Dorrie left to take a job in a shipyard in Brooklyn. She made twice as much money as I did as an assistant editor. Several times she came to visit us, and each time she practically gloated about her paychecks, her benefits, her holidays. Then one day, six months after leaving, she returned with her flowered suitcase.

"That girl isn't keeping him clean," she said, setting down the case too hard. "Look at his scalp. It's crusty."

"That's cradle cap, it isn't dirt."

"Never used to have it when I was here."

"What happened?"

"Nothing happened. Won't that girl you hired do windows?" She ran her finger over the windowsill.

"Dorrie, sit down and stop all this nonsense. You've quit your job, haven't you? Why?"

"Them sons a bitches can build their goddamned ships without me, that's why. Put me in another department. Filthy bloody dust everywhere and when I said where's m'mask, they said don't you know there's a war on and there's a shortage of stuff like masks, and I said to hell with the bloody dust, damned if I'd breathe in that filth all day, and they said okay, scram, or words to that effect."

"Well, there's no shortage of jobs now. You can get another one easily enough."

"I gave it a whirl, Emily, and I decided I don't like working. You're a number, someone to shove around, that's all. Who needs it? Get rid of that slut who's letting Scotty run around filthy dirty and I'll move back in."

"She doesn't let him stay filthy. And she's a very nice woman. You're used to more money than I can pay, you know."

"How much you have to pay that slut?"

"Twenty-five a week."

"M'God! For nothing! Let me fire her. I'll give her what for!"

And so Dorrie came back into our lives to stay.

"But it would be different now," I told her the next time the subject came up. "Surely you can see the advantages to having an education, getting a good job with a future? Not another backbreaking job in a factory."

"What future? You work so's you can buy a house, a car, furniture, and you get in debt, worry about payments, scrounge for bargains in silverware and dishes, junk like that. And when you get old you find you don't need all that house, or can't keep it up, and you sell it, or lose it one way or another. You can't drive the car no more, and you don't need the furniture in the tiny flat you can afford. What future?"

"It isn't like that with everyone. You could work, save your money, invest it, and when you are old you will be well provided for, not have to worry."

"Honey, I don't have to worry now."

"But you could make so much more money than I can afford to pay you."

"You hear me complaining? You want to fire me, just haul off and fire me, Emily, but no lectures first, no it's-for-your-own-good crap, okay?"

Later, when I had decided to buy the house, if she would stay with me, I brought up her future for the last time. "You've got Jimmie now, and he's wild about you. Why don't you go ahead and marry him and settle down?"

"With Jimmie?" She laughed raucously. "Let me tell you something, Emily. You have a gentleman friend and let him come calling, and he's made outa pure gold, couldn't be finer. Little presents. Takes you dancing, or the movies. You know. Holds the door open, brings you your tea. And you do things for him, make special strawberry pies, or keep rum on hand because he likes a spot now and then. It's nice. Polite like. But you marry him and pretty soon he starts grunting and groaning and carrying on about his back and his hard work and the bills and starts to complain about the food and you're spending too much money, you think he's made outa money? And he gets tired at eight and hates dancing and there's never a movie he wants to see anymore. They don't make them like they used to, now it's all trash. Too many people gets married that shoulda stayed single and happy. That's my opinion."

When we moved, her only comment about the house was, "God almighty! I'll tell you this, Emily. It's downhill all the way for this place, unless you come into a lot of money, hire a lot of people to keep fixing things when they go wrong, keep cleaning all the time, day after day. Downhill, that's its future."

Its shabbier than it was then, and getting shabbier every day, and it never is sparkling clean throughout. She cleans every room once a week, but from one week to the next dust collects, and spots appear, and no one can expect her or any other one person to keep up with the chores. Sometimes guilt overtakes me and I start waxing furniture, or washing windows, but then the phone rings, or someone comes by and I have to stop, and forget the house again until guilt forces it back to the front of my consciousness. The kids, the others who live there, help when they have time and think of it. Each one is responsible for his or her own room anyway, but Dorrie does the rest, and she has come to love/hate the house passionately.

"It reminds me of death and all that," she said once, throwing down a mop on the kitchen floor. "It's dying and I'm trying to keep it alive until it's an obsession with me. Fix the plaster in the dining room, patch the wallpaper in the hall, fix the stair treads where they are worn through. . . . Every day it's something different and I think, No, by God, you're not going to die under my care."

But it is dying, or maybe this quake finished it off and it lies in ruins, smoldering, hissing, a jet of smoke and fire erupting, but feebly, sinking down once more. I would rather see it die violently than have to sell it again, allow indifferent people to tramp through, testing the banisters, sniffing at the basement for mold, calculating the cost of replacing the furnace, pretending not to notice the missing plaster in the dining room, the cracked pane of glass in the kitchen.

I'm back to all that. I didn't send my mind far enough away. I remember the colonel's advice about how to solve a problem. It was during the period when the blacklisting Commie sniffers were at my heels. "You study it from every angle you can," he said. "Really dig for information, possibilities, possible approaches that no one else ever thought of, until you're saturated with it, until there's nothing anyone can bring up concerning it that you're not a better authority about, and then if you don't have the answer, forget it. Go fishing, if you're of that inclination. Go dancing. Read a good mystery novel. Try to imagine yourself as queen of England, or on the moon. Become a movie buff for a while. Sleep on it. If there's a solution, it'll come to you. But, Emily, sometimes there just ain't none, and if that's the case, that'll come to you too. And be ready to accept it if that is the case."

6

My father returned to New York in 1900, rented an apartment, and wrote a book about geology, scorning the old theories, mocking the old geognosts who sat in comfortable arm chairs and spouted about the creation of the earth, about mountain forming and volcanoes and strata. Then, manuscript ready, he looked over the list of publishers and chose Hamilden and McGowan, because he liked the sound of the name. He took a hansom cab to the offices on Delancey Street and there he met George De-Witt McGowan, the junior partner of the firm.

McGowan didn't like the book, but he liked William and the two became friends. "William," he said late one night, after a round of dinner, gambling, and a visit to a house he knew, "this life will kill both of us. Why don't you go home?"

William agreed solemnly that he should go home. "But I have to rewrite my book first."

"Take my advice, my friend, and do not rewrite the book. In fact there are some people who should never write books. You know why? They don't know books are alive, that's why. Think they're dead, inanimate things, and they aren't. Alive, books are, alive as much as you, I, that horse pissing away over there."

It was very late and there were few others out on the streets at that hour; the two men walked arm in arm, dressed in long coats, polished boots, high hats, talking drunkenly. A hansom clattered by and left deeper silence.

"Take me," McGowan went on. "Fourteen, worked in a print shop, can set type along with the best of them. Sixteen, worked in a bindery. Nineteen, came with Hamilden, and now, twenty-one, a publisher. Spent my whole inheritance to buy a partnership in publishing. Because I understand books and writers and love them both. Love them, William. Books and writers. Work from seven to seven, that's what I do. Seven to seven. Seven to three on Saturdays. Read a million words a month, five million, who knows how much? And sometimes a real writer shows up and I sniff him out, recognize him by the smell, the way he uses words, like living organisms, to be treated with respect. Worries about commas, about using *the* or *a*, about endings . . . word endings, I mean. They don't always worry enough about story endings, and I can understand that, it's because the story never ends, not if it's real and good. Not for some writers."

A hansom cab pulled abreast and the driver leaned over and asked if they wanted to ride.

"Where we going?" McGowan asked.

"To the park?"

They got in and the driver turned the horse and they were driven to Central Park, where they started the walk over again toward William's apartment on Fiftieth Street.

"No business," William said aloud, continuing a silent monologue he had begun in the cab. "Don't trust business, no business sense."

"No business," McGowan agreed. "Coming thing is corporations, no place for prospectors. Have to build you a corral." They both laughed immoderately. "Can't incorporate publishing, thank you kindly, God. Not a business, can't make committee decisions about books, thank you, God. One man, one writer, one book, that's the only way."

William yawned. "No business," he mumbled once more. "No books."

"Teach, that's what. Get married, have a family. Work for the United States Geologic Survey. That's for you.

Dig, measure mountains, maybe find more gold. That's the ticket for you, William."

On that drunken walk William's future was decided. McGowan introduced him to eligible girls in the weeks that followed, and one of them was Judge Randolf's daughter, Lorna.

Colonel McGowan told me years later that Judge Randolf was as crooked as an old apple tree, that there was a quiet investigation being made that year when my father met my mother, but no one knew anything of it, not even Lorna.

Lorna believed her father had taken an instant liking to the shy, gentle man from California; this was the first suitor the judge hadn't driven off one way or another. It was more likely that the judge, realizing the seriousness of the investigation concerning some of his decisions, thought his daughter might need the protection and comfort of a mature and well-to-do husband.

Having the judge's tacit approval filled Lorna's heart with joy, for she had fallen in love with William almost instantly. And he loved her dearly from the start.

Lorna was dainty and pretty, soft-spoken, with large blue eyes and dark brown hair. She was a fair musician, played the piano and violin, neither very well, but with passion. She wrote bad poetry and loved verse that was sentimental and flawlessly rhymed. She was an expert horsewoman, having grown up on the farm where the judge bred horses for the stables of New York and Philadelphia clientele. When her mother died, Lorna was eighteen and became mistress of her father's house; after she and William were married, they remained there for four years.

Willian didn't like horses. He rode—it was taken for granted that everyone rode—but, he said, he would never go out of his way looking for a horse to ride. And his conversations about horses consisted of verification that the animal in question was indeed a horse. He was bored with the Pocono Mountains, and the Taconics, and the Blue Ridge Mountains. Furry green hills he called them. He longed for California; he was homesick.

"I can't," Lorna said tearfully, nursing their child, Randolf. "Don't you see? It would kill Daddy for me to leave him now, so soon after Mother's death. I'm all he has."

And later: "Darling, please don't ask. Not now, not with

this scandal hanging over poor Daddy. They're trying to destroy him. Someone has to stick by or they'll think he really is guilty. How would it look if his only daughter left now?"

Wanda, their second child, was born, and William became more desperate to leave the judge's house. The two men could not talk for more than five minutes without arguing. William was strongly in favor of the People's Party and the land reforms they proposed. He believed the monopolistic railroads were a menace to the nation. He believed in unlimited coinage of silver, lower interest rates for farmers, an end to the land speculation that was raging in the West. He despised the growing corporations and feared their power. The judge thought he was a dangerous radical.

"Hell, we got to protect Americans! That's what the tariff act's about, you fool! And the Sherman Act is unconstitutional! Let them take a few cases to the Supreme Court and we'll see who's right! Let them demand my resignation, let them try to impeach me, we'll see! By God, they can't pass unconstitutional laws and expect honest judges to abide by them!"

But they passed the laws and those judges who didn't abide by them were often investigated and asked to resign or face impeachment. It was a new time, a time for reform; Teddy Roosevelt was in the saddle and whipping the horse, and judges like Melvin Randolf were on notice.

In November of 1903 he resigned, in order, he said, to devote more time to his other interests, including his horse farm. He closed his office in Philadelphia and retired to the farm.

"I can't stand it!" William said a month later to Lorna. They were in their bedroom, the only room in the house where they could talk. The judge seemed to be everywhere else, no matter the hour. 'I want to take you and our children and go home. This is no way to live, a guest in another man's house."

She wept, but in the end agreed. Even she could see that the two men could not live together now; the judge was bitter and harangued day and night about the ruination of the country that he foresaw. He and Willian no longer tried to talk; they shouted at each other, or maintained a cold silence; and the children were fearful of their grandfather's outbursts of profanity.

"Daddy, I'll come home every summer, I promise. We'll spend months and months with you each year. And you must come visit us in California."

She always believed his ruin was a political ploy. She refused to consider the evidence, or read the newspaper accounts of his misfeasance in office. Politics, she said, dismissing it all.

William's fortune had diminished to an alarmingly small figure by then, and he used what was left to buy back the house and furnish it once more as it had been during his childhood. He applied and was accepted by the United States Geologic Survey, and he was appointed professor at the University of San Francisco. All his life, every step of the way had been leading him to this goal, he realized.

Lorna was impressed by the house and enjoyed San Francisco life. She was lively and quick, and the pace here, so unlike Philadelphia, excited her. She liked the waterfront and the fish stalls, and the operas that came to town regularly, and the concerts, and the academic people who came to call. She was pregnant again and happy about that.

They dressed to attend the opera that April night in 1906. Caruso was to sing and Lorna was thrilled at the thought of seeing him in person. She had his records, of course, and played them over and over. She glittered in her mother's jewelry, and looked flushed and charming in her long dress designed to emphasize her high full bosom and hide her fuller belly. The baby was due in six weeks and this would be her last outing. They would have supper at the Palace Hotel after the opera, and then go to the Wilmingtons' party. She would not dance, of course, but she would be there with the others, and maybe Caruso would appear briefly, perhaps speak to her. . . .

William watched her pat her hair, touch her eyebrows with a wet finger, and, laughing, kissed her head. "You're more beautiful than ever," he said. "Pregnancy is most becoming to you, Mrs. Krump."

"Do I show very much?" she asked, standing, turning slowly before him.

"What you show will make every man who sees you mad with lust," he said.

She blushed, pleased, and they left in the new motor car they had bought to celebrate their fifth anniversary. Going down the hill, he narrowly missed one of Pulaski's goats, and he cursed it roundly. He and Pulaski had had words about the goats on a number of occasions; the animals kept the whole northern slope denuded and William was afraid of erosion, having recently read a persuasive article on the subject, but Pulaski merely shrugged, promised to keep them penned in, and forgot the matter until William brought it up again. There were few houses on the upper hill, but as they went down, there were more and more until they were in the city proper, where horse-drawn traffic was heavy and slow. Motor cars were still a rarity that drew crowds who gaped and laughed as William drove carefully, alert for holes, for rubble in the street that might give Lorna a bounce.

They hired a boy to watch the automobile near the theater, and joined the overflow crowd. The holiday atmosphere was quickened with pride that San Francisco had lured the greatest singer of all times, pride in the ornate Palace Theater, the grandest west of the Mississippi, pride in the wealth of the patrons, evidenced by the jewelry and fine furs.

The night was a spectacular success for everyone—for Caruso, who never sang better, nor to a more appreciative audience, and for the audience, which was uplifted, which felt a collective transcendence that lingered long after the music was silenced.

William and Lorna didn't go to the party; after their supper with friends, she was too tired to finish out the night, and they drove home slowly, speaking little, still in the spell of exquisite music. Lorna sighed often and her expression was dreamy as she prepared for bed, after checking on the children.

A sound like a ground-level thunderstorm awakened them; it was followed almost instantly by a violent shaking of the house, and an increase in the noise until it was as if a steam engine were driving down on them, or cannons thundering at them. William was on the floor, with no memory of getting there; Lorna was half on him.

"What is it?" Lorna screamed, clutching him.

He held her hard and waited. The house shuddered, something fell and broke with a crash, windows were tinkling, some of them breaking; one of the children began to scream, then the other; there was a last hard shudder and another crash from downstairs, and then the house quieted, the rumbling passed by, and it was over. Only then did William release Lorna, whom he had nearly smothered, holding her so tightly against his chest.

He jumped up, raced down the hallway and snatched up the children, one under each arm, and ran back to the master bedroom, where Lorna was struggling to her feet awkwardly. "Here, stand in the doorway!" William yelled, and deposited Randolf on the floor, kept Wanda under his arm, and hauled Lorna to the doorway just as the wave of aftershock came.

The noise was different this time, a rolling howl of discordant screeches, stone on glass, rocks being wrenched with shrill protests. . . . William could almost feel the tensions building in the house as wood twisted, strained, then miraculously was released and sprang back into place; popping, cracking, explosive rebounds echoed from each floor, each beam, joist, floorboard. It was over.

"Take them to bed and stay there with them," William said, and hurried Wanda to the bed while Lorna carried Randolf. "I'll see what it was." He met Bella, the housemaid, in the hall and together they ran through the house, inspecting the damage, carrying lanterns because the lights were out. Thank God, he breathed in the kitchen after his first check. Windows, some dishes, pottery, a lamp, the fireplaces, probably the chimneys, nothing that couldn't be repaired. "See if you can get coffee, will you," he said to Bella. "I'll go tell Mrs. Krump it isn't serious." He was faint with relief. He returned to Lorna, who was rigid, hardly breathing, clutching a child in each arm.

"It's all right," he soothed her, stroking her forehead, her cheek. She stared at him, too wide-eyed, ghastly white. "Relax now, Lorna," he said, speaking quietly, fear mounting as she continued to stare unblinkingly. "Just relax now. It's all over. No damage at all to speak of. It's all right."

Randolf stared at him, his thumb in his mouth, whimpering now and again, not moving. Wanda was asleep. He lifted her and put her back in her own bed, then lay down by Lorna and put his arm about her and his son. "It's all over now, Lorna. Try to sleep some more, it's too early to get up."

She closed her eyes but didn't relax, and when he moved she opened her eyes just as wide as before and drew her breath in sharply.

"I'll bring you coffee," he said. "You stay here and rest.

I'll be right back. Come on, Randolf. Want to see what Bella's doing?"

Randolf clung to his mother and started to cry again, and Lorna held him tightly, her eyes open, staring straight ahead.

"All right," William said. "You stay here with your mother. I'll be right back."

In the kitchen Bella was sweeping up glass. "The stove came on and went right off again," she said, "and I was afraid gas was leaking, so I made a fire in the dining-room fireplace and I've got the pot in there, if that's all right. It's smoking some, not too bad."

"Good, good. You're right about gas. I'll turn it off at the main. Leave the stove alone until I have a chance to get to town and see how much damage was done. My wife's in a bad state, Bella. I'm going to bring Randolf down to you. See that she rests, will you. I'm going to dress and go down to see how things are."

The coffee was bitter, but hot and strong, and after Lorna had sipped hers she was willing to release Randolf, who screamed with rage as he was hauled off to the kitchen, where Bella took him.

"Will you be all right?" William asked Lorna as he dressed. "Are you in pain?"

She shook her head. "The bed was rocking," she said. "It was going up and down, from side to side. It was, wasn't it, William?"

He nodded. "I'm going down to see how bad things are. I'll be right back. You stay in bed until I get back. Mrs. Sing will be here in a few minutes, and Bella is in the kitchen with Randolf. She'll get Wanda dressed when she wakes up. You just stay here and rest."

Lorna was staring again, pressing down with both hands on the bed.

"It's over, darling. It won't move again. There may be a few aftershocks, but they won't be bad, not serious. It's over now."

Later he realized that if she was in a state of shock that paralyzed her and then precipitated labor, he was in shock just as deep, but that took a different direction. He became hyperactive, and didn't stop all day. His mood ran from elation over being on the spot during what had to be the greatest earthquake of the century, and fear for the safety of his wife and family. Throughout the day he was in and out of town, asking questions, making observations, jotting notes, finding himself drafted to work on a fire team, watching the rescue efforts, taking part in them. Only that night when he stood in his own yard and looked out over the devastated city did he realize what the fires meant. The pall of smoke and dust hung everywhere, glowing a dirty orange that flared here, then there, dulled momentarily, flared even brighter. . . . They wouldn't be able to put them out. There was not enough equipment, no water, and a strong wind. The fires would rage until rain came or they burned themselves out.

He had read about the great fire of London, about the repeated burnings of Chicago, about the fire storms that raced through the dry north woods, and he knew what fire in that tinderbox city meant, and he knew there was no place he could take his wife, who was moaning with labor pains by then, and his infant children.

He returned to the house. The water had failed early that day, and from Pulaski's well he had collected what he could in buckets, had filled a barrel, the three bathtubs, pots, pans, pails, but it wouldn't be enough if the fire came up the hill. Lorna screamed and he clenched his fists until they hurt. Mrs. Sing was with her, and had chased him away, muttering unintelligibly at him, scowling. Mrs. Sing was Chinese, smooth-faced, with a family that included children and grandchildren, and he couldn't judge her age at all. But she knew about childbirth, about premature babies, she had said when he failed to return with a doctor. She knew, she take care, he stay away. He went to the yard once more and stared at the burning city until his eyes felt afire. Out here he could no longer hear Lorna's screams.

William believed in heaven and hell and eternal damnation, but hell had no power over him after the three days that followed. He had been to hell and survived, he thought later. Lorna descended into hell and didn't survive. Her body recovered slowly, but Lorna never came back to him.

Pulaski's goats had saved the hill, he admitted, and still cursed them for denuding the slopes for the next few years until Pulaski moved his family, goats, chickens, dogs, and rabbits out of the city to the country. As Lorna withdrew more and more, William became involved with city politics, joined efforts to rewrite the buildling code, make the city safe from earthquake damage, and after ten years of that, gave up, and concentrated on his classes and his summer field trips. Each year as soon as school was out, Lorna gathered the children, trunks, suitcases, boxes, and went to the judge's farm, where she stayed until fall. William joined them one time, then refused, pleading work.

Their home life had changed dramatically after the earthquake. Lorna took a different bedroom; she was restless and fearful if the bed moved during the night, and William threw himself about so. There was no question of sex anymore—her health had been affected, she had become too delicate, another pregnancy might kill her. There was no medical opinion; it was given as a statement of fact, accepted by William, who felt he was to blame for the premature birth, for the terrible ordeal Lorna had suffered, for the earthquake, everything.

The children grew up unnoticed for weeks at a time, undisciplined, cautious in their mother's presence, because they might make her become faint, or have a debilitating headache that would keep her in her darkened room for days. In the evenings William worked in his study, which opened to the terrace; Lorna sat in the small drawing room doing needlework, or sometimes played the piano in the formal living room, or supervised the lessons of one or another of the children.

William often took the three children to the beach where they hunted agates and shells and starfish in the tide pools. He took them into the hills and they tried to find gold in the streams. He built them a treehouse in an oak tree behind their house, and there were trails through the woods still on the hill, where they could play Indian games. Without exception they all hated their visits to Judge Randolf's farm each summer.

"You're going to be a lawyer, aren't you, young man? Aren't you?" The old man was fiercer than ever. He had lost a lot of money in his fight to save his job and reputation; his horses were not selling well since everyone wanted motor cars, which he hated passionately. His horses were no good for racing, they were riding horses, or horses bred to look handsome pulling a carriage. Some of his former cronies were turning against him, demanding repayment of money he had considered gifts, which they were now calling loans. Lorna returned her mother's jewelry to him and it vanished; he questioned her intently about William's financial status, and was sarcastic and cruel about William in front of the children, calling him a threadbare schoolmaster.

He made them learn to ride, watching their progress with a long stick in his hand, which he used to swat them with sharply when they slumped or didn't hold their heads just right. He made the girls use sidesaddles and they hated every minute of it. He planned Randolf's career from the start, picked the schools, the age at which he would enter boarding school in Philadelphia, where he could keep an eye on him, everything to do with his future.

"Why haven't you taught those girls to do needlework?" he demanded of Lorna one afternoon. "Why aren't they taking music lessons?"

Lorna bowed her head and mumbled something about William not thinking it necessary if they didn't want to, and he raged for an hour. The next day he had a violin teacher for Randolf and a woman who sat with the girls and made them stitch on tea towels until their fingers bled.

"I'll never come back here," Emily sobbed that night, huddled close to her older sister. "I'll run away first!"

"Me too," Wanda whispered, but her voice quavered, and they both knew she would not protest beyond the bedroom walls. Wanda was like Lorna, fearful of bringing down the wrath of her mother, her grandfather, more afraid of the displeasure of the adults about her than of the pinpricks and the discomfort of learning to ride sidesaddle. Perhaps there was a dim memory of the time when Lorna had been gay and happy, loving and warm, and there was a vague, never-voiced hope of having that time return. Each day she bent her head dumbly over the needlework—embroidery, crochet, knitting, tatting, needlepoint, hemming with invisible stitches, darning. . . .

"I won't," Emily said after two days. She put the towel with its uneven hem down carefully on the table and sat back in her chair, her feet swinging clear of the floor, and stared defiantly at Mrs. Caprioni.

"Look at it, Emily. How ragged those stitches are! The hem must be straight and smooth, the stitches small and neat. Now, be a dear and rip them out and try once more."

"I won't."

"Dear, your grandfather will be very displeased. Young ladies are expected to be accomplished in the womanly graces of needlework. How will you ever find a man to marry you if you can't do a simple thing like hemming a tea towel? You will be an old maid with no one to love you, no children to play at your feet, alone and lonely. . . ."

"I don't care! I won't get married! I'll never get married!"

Wanda looked from the heavy woman to the thin child without raising her head, her fingers stilled, waiting for the outcome of this rebellion. She was frightened.

"Emily, I insist that you stop this intemperate display of willfulness and resume your lesson!" Mrs. Caprioni's voice was that of a teacher who would put up with nonsense only so long. Emily stiffened and shook her head. "Very well. Come with me." She took the child's arm in a firm grip and pulled her from the chair. "Wanda, I expect you to have that hem finished when I return."

From somewhere in the house came the sound of a wailing violin; outside, the sun shone brightly and foals pranced in lush fields; in the living room, Judge Randolf made notes from his own case decisions and Lorna sat nearby, contentedly embroidering a pillow case. When Mrs. Caprioni knocked, then entered, half dragging the reluctant child along with her, neither the judge nor his daughter welcomed the intrusion into a moment that had somehow become time long since gone.

"Well?" the judge said harshly, impatiently, not even looking at the child.

"Emily is being willful and disobedient, sir," Mrs. Caprioni said. "She will not do her sewing."

"Well, whip her," the judge said, and returned to the work on his desk.

Emily looked desperately toward her mother, but Lorna was intent on her work and didn't glance up. Mrs. Caprioni nodded, turned, and dragged the child out with her. She made Emily go with her to the willow tree near the creek and watch as she cut a switch and trimmed it, tried it through the air, making it whistle. They went to Emily's room and Mrs. Caprioni switched her bared buttocks.

The next day Emily refused to pick up the hated tea

towel, and Mrs. Caprioni switched her again and left her in her room while Wanda had her lessons.

On the fourth day Emily vomited when it was time to report to Mrs. Caprioni, and for several days she was allowed to remain in her room while the sewing lessons took place. When Mrs. Caprioni came the following Monday, she vomited again; Lorna wept and the judge cursed and called Emily her father's daughter, but after that no one tried to make her learn to stitch, crochet, knit, darn. . . . While Wanda learned the womanly graces, Emily stayed in her room and read happily.

If the judge had not disliked her before, it became clear that after this incident he had taken a definite position concerning his youngest grandchild. She had nearly cost him his beloved daughter, he said scathingly, and she had the devil in her and was a bad influence on the other children, who were well behaved and obedient. The radicalism of the father showed in the child, he said, but thank God it was in a girl, not in Randolf.

Lorna reported the matter to William when they returned home in the fall. "You just don't understand how difficult it is for me to manage the children all summer," she said. "I come home exhausted and find you have invited students to stay here. It isn't fair." She told on Emily, to illustrate the problems she encountered that he was ignorant of.

"You let that woman whip our child! You and that sadistic old man!"

"For heaven's sake, William! A whipping never hurt a child! She was deliberately disobedient."

"She won't go back. I'll keep her with me if you insist on going back there, but Emily will never go back to that house! And neither will Randolf or Wanda if either of them objects. And Randolf will not go to a boarding school in Philadelphia! That old man is not running my family!"

Lorna clutched her breast and fell back into her chair, but William didn't seem to notice. He stamped from the room, slamming the door behind him.

Randolf and Wanda never objected aloud to him, although they muttered to each other about refusing to go back to the farm, about running away, about setting their mouths and saying "I won't!" the way Emily had done. In the end, the two older children did none of those things and suffered their summers silently, but Randolf did not go to boarding school and he did not study law.

When William died suddenly in 1932, Lorna moved back to her father's farm. The judge was very old and feeble then. They were both happy until he died two years later and it was discovered that he had mortgaged the farm, that he had sold all his stocks and bonds, everything in the almost-forgotten fight to stay out of prison. The Depression had ruined William, too, and Lorna was left at fifty-six a widow, penniless, with no skills except needle-work.

7

"Come on, Scotty, this way!" I ran toward the cliffs ahead of him; he was as excited now as I was, although he didn't yet know why. We had to pick our way down with care and we could not see the ocean, but it was there pounding, and the smell of salt air was exhilarating. At the foot of the cliff I started to run again, braked by the drifted sand and the strong sea breeze. Scotty passed me, laughing. We came out from behind the rocks that had screened the ocean from view and suddenly Scotty stopped. He had seen the shore in New Jersey, where the water was dull brown with silt, the waves feeble, many people bathing, and this was not that ocean. Here the ocean was untouched, clean, and the waves were supreme, crashing with thunderous impact against the cliffs that curved down to the water's edge, crashing down on the shore with explosive force, shooting sprays twenty feet or higher where the waves broke against boulders. I had stopped, there was no one in sight, only my small son, and the sea and the beach as it had existed from day one on the geologic clock. I wanted to weep and didn't know why. Without warning, Scotty started to spin around, flinging his hands outward, whirling, whirling, faster and faster, close to the foaming water, then farther away, and I heard myself saying, "He's dancing to celebrate life."

I didn't recognize the words, didn't remember hearing them before when I had spun around to relieve an intolerable burden of emotion. He came speeding back to me and caught my hand and together we ran down the beach, leaving deep prints in the wet, packed sand until, exhausted, we fell down and tried to catch our breath.

I wonder if Scotty remembers. When I get out of here, when he comes flying out to visit me, a duty visit, I'll remind him and I'll suggest he try to see that boy, reach out to him, reassure him. It helps, I'll tell him. I can see myself sitting in a chair that is uncomfortably high, my feet swinging, starting to tingle in the first stages of going to sleep, that goddamned tea towel on my lap, forgotten as I watch a drop of blood on my finger growing larger and larger.

I can view her/me with love and pity now, and I want to tell her, you don't have to take this crap! Don't let them do this to you!

I keep dozing and dreaming, coming wide awake to listen for sounds of people digging, shouting, gunning motors, anything. There isn't anything.

I am walking down a dark narrow street, there are tall buildings, no lights on anywhere. The street dead-ends ahead of me at an intersecting cross street; a pale light from the left keeps it from being totally black where the two streets come together. There is a faint wind, not enough to blow my hair, but it must be stronger on the cross street: I can hear an empty can clattering. I walk slower and slower, in great dread, but without a cause I can name. No one else is in sight, there is no traffic, no one but me and the dead city, the black buildings, the blacker windows where no eye watches my progress. Sometimes a paper stirs, but not enough to rustle or move away; it stirs, as if testing invisible restraints, finds them impossible, and falls softly to the street. It is very dirty: papers, bottles, overturned garbage cans, discards—a shoe, a bit of a towel, a dead dog. I can see these things quite well although it is dark. The dog is a red cocker puppy, with white streaks on his breast. I stop near it, not looking at it, looking the other way in fact, but I see it. Its eyes are open. It sees me. Now my dread becomes terror and I run toward the end of the street where there is light from a distant source.

Things are piled up before the dim buildings, heaps of things I can't identify, not cans or crates. I can't tell what they are, and they stretch out of sight in both directions. I seem no closer to the cross street, even though I have been running so long that my legs are throbbing, and my heart feels as if each beat might make it explode in a bloody eruption. I can't get enough air. Now the darkness expands, then contracts to a point like a giant eye adapting to light and dark.

Suddenly I am at the corner and I stop in icy panic, unable to move, to scream, to look away. Against the building, the objects I perceived as stacks of things are people—men, women, children—sitting with their backs against the brownstones and concrete and iron railings. They don't move. They are as gray as the buildings, as silent, as uninhabited. Their eyes are lusterless black holes in deep pits. This is the blackness that expands, that I drown in; their eyes blink, and the blackness is a point only.

They are drawing me across the street, and I cannot resist. I know the darkness has closed in behind me, that the street I was on has been swallowed by it; I know the light source is receding, fading, the illumination from it is perceptibly dimmer, gray-blue; I know if I permit myself to be forced down against that cold empty building, I will never get up.

"No!"

The sound of my scream shocks me wide awake, banishes the images. What was that? I don't know, and am willing to call it a dream, but I don't feel it was a dream. It had the gritty feel of realism that is lacking in dreams. The future? If so I reject it; I won't have such a future. I refuse it, and even as I think these thoughts, I know that those people huddled against the buildings will exist in some kind of future. I feel it as surely as I feel that the past I am reexperiencing here this night has shaped this present, that if any one element of it had been different, I would be somewhere else now, or dead. But, more, there is a way I can help that child I was, help her survive the many traumas and terrors of childhood, help her to grow up not too frightened, strengthened by a touch she can never understand. The companion thought is too frightening to dwell on: is there a way one can reach into a dimly perceived future to order change there?

I am very thirsty, and I find that strange. I never awaken in the night wanting a drink of water, wanting to go to the bathroom, and now I want both. That street has reminded me of something, not the street itself, because I never saw a New York street so barren and empty, but the feel of hopelessness and despair that permeated the street, that I have known before.

The apartment I lived in when I worked with Jason left a few very clear images in my memory. I remember the table: it wobbled until he folded a piece of paper and put it under one leg; the two-burner gas stove top and the sofa where I slept are precise, intact memories. Mother had the other room with the narrow bed. The table was covered with linoleum, regular floor linoleum, that had blue flowers on a black background. There was a round sink and narrow drainboard; the sink had a permanent yellow-gray stain, the porcelain was chipped in four spots. The apartment was in a tenement on East Twelfth Street.

Every day I walked downtown to make the rounds of the half dozen publishers who sometimes gave me work—copy editing or occasionally a rewrite job, or the chance to sub for a reader who was off, or help with other office work on an hourly basis, enough to get out a mailing, or to catch up with correspondence. If I got a job that day, I rode the subway home; otherwise, I walked both ways.

I left my last prospect, and stood blinking in the cold air on Fifth Avenue, dreading the long walk. I had calluses on the soles of my feet from too-thin shoes, and my coat was not warm enough; the snow flurries looked more determined to become real snow than they had earlier in the day. I bowed my head against the wind and started.

"Emily!"

I thought I had imagined it. I was light-headed from a day without food and a slug of gin that Gloria Woodson had given me along with the bad news that they had nothing for me.

"Emily!" Again. Closer this time. I couldn't see past the mass of bodies, all bundled up in gray and black and mud-colored winter clothing. Someone caught my arm and pulled me free of the other people, into a doorway, out of the wind.

"Maury! It is you, isn't it? Maury!"

And right there in front of all those people, we kissed. I don't think anyone even noticed.

"I wrote and the letter came back. I thought you had gone home. Are you all right?"

"I thought you were in Washington."

"Where can we talk?"

"I have to go home. Mother's living with me now. She'll worry."

"Let me come with you. I have to talk to you. You're thin."

"Fashionably slender, you mean. Come on. Let's walk."

I had a twenty-dollar check in my purse that I couldn't cash at that time of day, the last one I would have in God alone knew how long, but I didn't have a nickel for a cup of coffee or the subway. I would have suggested coffee, or something, if I had been able to pay my own way. You never knew with anyone those days how broke they were. We walked.

"Where have you been? Why did my letter come back?"

"Father died. I had to go. They were ruined, along with everyone else. I must have been in California."

"But you're working? You're okay?"

"I'm okay. I'm free-lance editing. What are you doing?"

"I'm working for the Roosevelt administration. He's doing it, Emily, just as he promised! We're changing the country! Bringing back hope and faith in the future. And it will spread, cover the whole world. It really is a New Deal!"

I clenched my fists. "But what are you doing in New York?"

"Trying to peddle a book. This fellow, Jason Mohr, has written a brilliant analysis of Roosevelt's accomplishments and his goals, the goals for the whole country. Not propaganda," he added hastily. "He's not connected in any way with the administration. He's a doctoral candidate at Columbia and we—I—believe the book should have a regular publisher, not be buried in a university press. I thought because I know a few people I could handle this, but I was wrong."

"If it's good—" I started. He stopped me.

"That's the problem, apparently. It isn't good. It's brilliant, an intellectual accomplishment, but pretty rough reading."

"Oh."

"What does that mean? Oh."

"I've seen those things before. If the university press is willing to publish, you'd better let them."

"No! I'm going to help him rewrite. . . ." He stopped walking and dragged me to a halt. "You could do it."

"Don't be an idiot. I'm not a writer."

"He doesn't need a writer. He needs an editor. The manuscript is seven hundred pages long, and in Germanic sentences."

"It sounds to me as if you've already had editorial opinions on the manuscript." The wind gusted harder and I shivered. The gin was wearing off. We were at Thirty-second Street, and all I could think of was Twelfth Street and hot soup.

"Read it. Do me a favor and just read it, Emily. If you say it's impossible, I'll believe you. Rubens didn't get all the way through, he admitted he didn't."

"Solly Rubens turned it down?"

"He didn't read it!"

"He probably didn't have to read it all the way through. Sometimes you don't."

Maury stopped me again and shook me. "And I say there is a gold mine in it! Do you think I'm stupid? I wouldn't be working like this for a piece of junk!" He let me go and I swayed a moment, but he didn't notice. "I would pay you. Not me personally, our publicity department, the Democratic party, it would come out of their funds. How much?" When I didn't answer, he said, "Is five hundred enough? Rubens said a professional ghostwriter would want a thousand at least, but I don't want it rewritten, just edited."

Thirty-first Street. A snow squall caught us on the corner, and from somewhere there was the smell of sausage. My knees felt weak. Five hundred dollars! "I'll read it, and I'll have to meet him, to see if we could possibly work together. I don't know, Maury. I've never done anything like this. I don't know anything about politics. . . ."

"That's why I don't want you to ghostwrite it, you or anyone else. He knows. I want what he has to say to be there, nothing else, but in English."

"That bad?"

Suddenly he pulled me around the corner and into a

hole-in-the-wall restaurant and I nearly fainted from the unexpected fragrances of hot food.

"Are you hungry?"

All I could do was laugh.

We ate, then took a cab to his hotel and got the manuscript. I wouldn't go to his room with him. I don't think he wanted me to. He had married Estelle, he said, when I returned his letter unopened, or when he thought I had returned it. She was sticking by him, although both families were furious with him for throwing away his future to work for That Man. Her parents wouldn't see him, or have anything to do with either of them. He was beautiful that night, enthusiastic, hopeful, fired with faith that balanced dangerously on the edge of fanaticism. We walked again and I listened to him from Forty-eighth Street to Twelfth Street, and we agreed to meet the next afternoon, when I would tell him my decision about the book.

Two days later I met Jason in the coffee shop of Maury's hotel, where I had three doughnuts and two milkshakes. Jason spilled a cup of tea and looked at the tabletop and at the ceiling and the floor and his hands and didn't look at me until we had been there for almost an hour. He was nearly six feet tall, as skinny as a skeleton wrapped in skin, and so nervous that I had to keep eating doughnuts so that I wouldn't twitch in sympathy. He was twenty-three. It was painful to draw anything at all from him. Each question raised a flush that swept over his face, then left so quickly that he looked dead by contrast. He was too pale, and his teeth were bad. His overcoat was too small for him, and his shoes were desperately shined over worn spots. They probably had holes the size of Roosevelt buttons.

"What are your hours?" I asked him. "We'll have to work out a schedule and go over the manuscript line by line. It's going to take time."

"Um, I have this class, three of them. And I'm studying myself. Um, there's my thesis I'm working on. And, uh, I teach. . . ."

It was like that for hours until we finally got it down on paper. We couldn't meet at his room, which he shared with another student-teacher graduate student. That left my apartment, and my mother, and I had to explain that, and he nodded at the ceiling and nearly knocked his water over. Maury caught the glass. When Jason finally left with my address written on a slip of paper, we both sighed. Maury said, "You're going to earn every penny. I'll see if I can get you more."

"He'll loosen up when we get to work," I said, and hoped I was right.

"It's good to see you again," Maury said then. He reached across the table and held my hand. "It's so good to see you again."

"I know." And I thought, If I had known he was willing to give up the prestigious position with the prestigious firm and the assured prestigious future, would I have sent him away? I didn't know. I don't know now.

The first two times Jason came to work, my mother stayed up until he left and never stopped watching us. The first night was agony; he glanced at the pages, then looked at the flowers on the linoleum tabletop, the walls, my mother's foot, his knuckles.

"You can't repeat the same things in the first four chapters," I said. "No one will keep reading. After you said it once, why did you say it over and over again?"

"Um, it's not exactly, that is, I, um . . ."

"Jason, I suppose it's important that you bring in the historical aspects of economical planning and I'll even grant that you have a reason to explain the Louisiana Purchase in some detail, but not for four chapters! At that rate you don't get to the present until page 200, and that's too damn late!"

My mother coughed. I glared at her.

"It's too damn late!" I said, louder.

Jason nodded, glanced at me and almost smiled, and nodded again. I grinned back at him and we went on.

We worked four nights a week, first going over the monster manuscript deciding where we could cut out a section, a page, a paragraph. Then we started on the syntax.

"You have to decide just who your audience is, Jason," I said on one of those nights. "If they are idiots, you can't give them this book at all. Write a primer, if that's who you're aiming at. If you think they have any intelligence, don't insult that intelligence by explaining over and over. I know, you're afraid if they don't follow your arguments step by step, they won't grant your conclusions or understand your concerns about the future. But they won't read it if you're this condescending."

And again. "My God, Jason, what does this sentence mean? What do these words mean? Where is the verb? What kind of syntax are you trying to invent?"

The sentence started: "The agglomeration of multipowers within a system where the concealment of the interconnecting hierarchical jurisdictional functions is the primary, even the efficient, antecedent goal in an *a priori* differentiation of departmental levels . . ." It never ended, but petered out somewhere near the bottom of the page.

"Mrs. Carmichael, if you don't like the book, why are you working so hard on it?" His voice was soft, with a slight drawl. He was from Illinois, by way of Brooklyn, where his father worked in a hat factory three days a week.

"I do like the book, Jason. I like it very much. I like what you finally say." I got up and made tea. He didn't drink coffee and because I didn't care and couldn't afford it anyway, I joined him in tea orgies those nights. Why was I working so hard? I hadn't thought of it. Not for the money, not really, although the five hundred dollars had been the incentive at first. I looked at him slouched at the table, staring at the sentence I had picked on, following it with a pencil, word for word, starting over, his lips moving, his thin face taut with concentration. He scribbled something on the page, then started at the top again, and I sighed. I thought that somehow I could see through him, that gangly boy with bad teeth and bad nerves, into a core of brilliance that was dazzling. His book was a mixture of oversimplified bad prose and overcomplex bad prose. But he wasn't interested in literature. He hadn't grasped yet that his special kind of brilliance had to be wrapped in words as elegant as his ideas were, as direct and simple and beautiful as the mind that conceived the ideas. His prose had erected barriers between his ideas and his readers.

I thought of a jeweler contemplating a raw diamond in matrix, not cut yet, not revealing a hint of the magical beauty that lay within the rock. The beauty reaches out to touch the jeweler, to give him courage to raise his tools, to strike, to cut and break the rock in order to reveal what he knows is there. Touched by beauty, his hand is guided by the promise and the limitations of the stone, and he is unable to draw back although he knows that the tools he uses to reveal beauty can also destroy it. He knows when he raises his hammer that he will be forgotten, that the cut diamond, the perfect facets, the flawless depths are what people will admire and remember; the owner and all subsequent owners are the ones who will reap the financial benefits, not the craftsman who released the spell, revealed the magic, but that won't be important. The moment the stone is cut, and light is caught, reflected back a thousandfold, that is the moment of fulfillment.

I took the tea to the table and sat down opposite Jason. He spooned sugar into his cup and stirred so hard that the tea flew out over the rim. He threw his spoon down and leaned back.

"That sentence says exactly what it means," he said sulkily. "You tell me not to explain too much, and then you pretend you can't understand, I think this whole thing is a mistake."

"And the book is bad and I'm a lousy editor and you'd do better just mailing the book around to publishers until it crumbles away to dust. . . ."

He glowered and sucked his lower lip.

"Tell me what you mean by the paragraph, starting with that one sentence."

He glanced at the page. "The agglomeration of multi—"

"Don't read it. I can do that. I can even pronounce the words. What do you mean?"

"You know exactly what I mean. You know every time you do this to me."

"Tell me."

"Any organization that gains enough power to control every phase of its functions threatens to become an uncontrollable monolithic system that will defy and frustrate any attempt at regulation by any outside force."

"Good boy," I murmured. I sipped my tea and watched him.

His hands shook when he lifted his cup. "It's all through it," he said, not looking at me. "You've known all along?"

"Yes. I read it, remember? Really read it."

"Mr. Farber doesn't know."

"No. I rather think he doesn't."

"Mrs. Carmichael, they won't like it when they understand it. And you're making me write it so they will understand."

"They'll like it. And businessmen will like it. The Republicans will love it, the Democrats will love it, the Communists will love it, fundamentalists . . . everyone will find in it something to condemn the enemy, whoever that enemy is. You've written a great book, Jason, and everyone is going to latch on to a small piece of it and think it's the whole thing. Can't you see them all, hanging on for dear life, each clutching one tiny strand, being carried along with all the others."

"You're mocking me now, aren't you?"

I shook my head. "I'm awed by you, I think. I don't understand you, how you think, who you are, what you are. I am not mocking you."

He blushed and stood up. "I'm glad you're making me do it right. I didn't realize how I was trying to hide. But I was, wasn't I? I was afraid they'd laugh at me, whoever *they* are. But you, you found me out right away, and you kept digging at me, digging, digging. I've been ready to strangle you, you know that, don't you? I've hated you!"

I laughed. "You aren't very good at hiding anything yet, you know."

He blushed again. Now he glanced at the bedroom door. My mother was in there sleeping. "Can you go out for a walk or something. Can we talk?"

It wasn't very cold that night, and we walked and he talked for hours. Downtown, uptown, Times Square, back to the Village. We stopped for coffee and found that neither of us had brought a cent, he because he didn't have it and I because I had forgotten my purse. We left the restaurant and walked some more.

I can't remember what he said. It was hopeful and full of despair; naïve and wise; elegant and coarse. He had had a vision during which he had seen a future that frightened him, and he was trying to reach into the future, change the shape of it before it solidified, and I believed he could do it with his book.

It was dawn when we got back to my apartment. "I have a class at eight," he said. Without warning he grabbed me, as a child grabs a coveted toy, and kissed me awkwardly. His fingers clutched, dug into my back, and his lips were cold and hard and moved in a strange way, as if he were trying to talk. Then he spun around and ran away down the street.

He never mentioned that kiss, and I wondered if he had

managed to wipe it from his memory. For a time he was
back to the "Um, er, that is" stage, but it didn't last, and
we made good progress.

We worked hard all spring, and it was telling on both of
us. Jason was teaching twenty-five hours a week, tutoring
on the side, working with me four nights, and he was writing his thesis. His major was history and he was extracting
sections of his book, adding other material, studying, reading, not sleeping enough, never eating enough. He chewed
his fingernails until his fingers bled, and drank rivers of
tea, and ran to the bathroom down the hall, and grew no-
ticeably thinner.

I worked on his book, typing final copy as we went
along; I was doing copy editing when I could get it,
putting in applications everywhere I could think of, seeing
people, waiting in lines for interviews, and I also became
thinner. I was obsessed with the need to make Jason's
book as perfect as possible, and I was more obsessed with
my own need to escape poverty. I was terrified that my
mother might become ill, that I might have an accident,
that I might not be able to pay the next month's rent, or
buy food the following week.

There were signs that I should have noticed, or should
have tried to do something about, and didn't. Sometimes
Jason would sit for hours without glancing at the work
spread on the table. "They'll never let it get through," he
said. "What's the use?"

"Who? What do you mean?"

"I only want to wake up a dozen people, no more than
that. Just a dozen. They won't let me. A dozen people can
make enough noise to wake up a hundred more, and it es-
calates from there until no one's sleeping. They know
that."

"Who, Jason? What are you talking about?"

"They won't bother you. You're just doing a job. If it
was about architecture, it would be all the same to you.
They'll understand that." He grinned at me suddenly and
said, in an absolute change of mood that was upsetting, "I
have a student, Ralph, about nineteen, and very fat. He
made a special belt that has a steel bearing right in the
middle and he can balance himself on that—you know,
feet, chest, arms all off the ground—and start spinning,
and he can keep it up indefinitely. Darnedest thing you

ever saw, fat Ralph spinning like a top. He's going to try to get on stage somewhere." He laughed hard.

He wasn't sleeping more than three or four hours a night, and often not that much, and he was convinced that the head of his department was somehow reading his thesis in progress.

School would soon be over, I told myself, often, when it began to bother me. School would be over and he would sleep normally, and live at home and eat regularly, and rest. And when the book was sold he could get his teeth fixed.

We finished the book and went together to the office where he was to deliver it for approval by the Democratic party, and then we walked silently, fearful now that it wasn't as good as we had thought, that the person who was to read it and pay me would be out of town—a girl had taken it, had said she would pass it along.

"It's juvenile," Jason said, slouching along, carrying his coat. It was very warm that day.

"I should have retyped parts of it again. God, I wish I were a better typist."

"Your parts are beautiful," he said. "You just can't make silk ears out of a sow's purse."

We were passing a dime store. "Come on," I said, laughing. "I'll treat you to jelly beans." I had a quarter and used five cents of it to buy jelly beans and we walked hand in hand eating them. Five hundred dollars, I kept thinking. I'd buy new shoes first thing, heavy shoes that would last and last and not hurt my feet. My mother wanted yarn and some patterns. Maybe Jason and I would see a movie, have dinner out to celebrate.

"Emily, who's that man following us?"

I was jolted from my pleasant reveries and looked around. "Who?"

"That old man in the tan pants, blue shirt. He's been behind us for blocks."

I saw the man then, nobody, a man. "So he has to go this way, too."

Jason shook his head. "They're having me followed," he said. "I suspected a long time, but never caught them before."

"Who's having you followed? Why would anyone?"

"You know." He glanced back and walked faster.

A week later he came to tell me he had lost his grant

and the university was cutting back on staff, they were sorry, it was no reflection on his abilities, they would give him the highest recommendations possible. . . .

"What will you do?"

"Go home, see if the hat factory needs anyone to work two days a week. I wouldn't want to deprive my father of his work."

"Jason, just hold on, will you? In a few days I'll go see Hanrahan and get my money, that will be enough to tide you over until you find a publisher and get an advance. I should have made two copies. We could have been circulating one to publishers by now."

There hadn't been enough money to buy top sheets for two copies, and we had been unwilling to submit carbons either to Mr. Hanrahan or to publishers.

"Listen," he said, and tiptoed to the door where he put his ear close to the wood and held his breath. There were only the usual tenement noises, cries, someone laughing, a baby crying. . . .

He jerked the door open, looked up and down the hall-way, then slammed it. "They're fast," he said.

"No one's out there."

He looked ill; he was ill. He had been pushing too hard, too long. He was not sleeping well, he told me, and there were dreams, terrible dreams. He would not tell me any of the dreams. And now, recently he had discovered that they were having him followed, his every movement was watched, and he was afraid. The room he shared with an-other graduate student, who also had been fired, was paid up through June, and after that they would have to leave and there was no place to go. Unless they snatched him, he said darkly.

"We'll know something before the end of the month," I said over and over. I called Mr. Hanrahan, but he was too busy to come to the phone and could I leave a message, he would return the call.

"To a corner pay phone?" I asked bitterly, and hung up.

Mother had begun to complain about the heat in the apartment, and it was unbearable, but there was nothing I could do about that. The one window was in her bedroom and she stayed in there with the door closed for hours at a time, hunched over needlework, or with a book of poetry on her lap, or a letter she was writing to Randolf, or just looking at nothing at all. She and Randolf wrote back and forth each week. She was waiting for him to get a full-time job, when she planned to move in with him and his wife and their two children. She thought the way I lived was shameful, indecent. Wanda and her husband were in even worse shape than Randolf; Wanda was having trouble with her health, asthma, then appendicitis, then something else, and something else. "Female troubles," my mother said, folding the letter from Wanda, tucking it into her pocket. She never showed me their letters, but referred to them as if I had read them.

"We'll move," I promised her. "As soon as I get paid. We'll move to a bigger apartment with more windows."

"This isn't fit for decent people." She sniffed. "I can't imagine why you rented it in the first place."

"It was all I could afford."

"If you would get a real job, stop this gallivanting around all the time looking for a place at the top, you'd be better off. If you won't live with your husband, you have to work, that's all there is to it."

I walked out as she talked. Five hundred dollars, I kept thinking. And better, I had proven I was an editor, a real editor, and now someone would know that and offer me a position with a good firm. Someone, Solly Rubens, perhaps, who had seen the manuscript before, would recognize the work that had gone into it shaping it up. . . .

Mr. Hanrahan's office was on Fifty-eighth between Seventh and Eighth avenues. There were three rooms, the connecting doors had been taken off the hinges and were stacked against the wall. The rooms were crowded, telephones were ringing, typewriters clattering, and over it all the beat of voices rose and fell like the surf.

"I'm looking for Mr. Hanrahan," I told a woman at a desk near the door.

"Jimmie! Someone for you!" she called over the din without looking up at me. Her head, bent as it was, revealed half an inch of black hair on both sides of the part; the rest was hennaed, and it was set in hard, tight waves.

I had to ask two more people before someone pointed him out to me. He was in one of the adjacent rooms, talking with two other men.

"Mr. Hanrahan?"

He glanced at me, took in the five-year-old dress, the scuffed shoes, my gloves, darned and frayed. "No jobs, sister. We're filled up. Sorry." He was a compact man, medium build with bright blue eyes and sandy hair and mustache. There were crinkle lines about his eyes as if he laughed often. He reminded me of my grandfather Randolf.

"It's not that," I said before he could turn back to his friends. "I'm Emily Carmichael, here about Jason Mohr's book. Mr. Farber said you'd read it, give it a recommendation. And give me a check."

"I'll get to it," he said, turning again to the other men.

"But you've had it three weeks! At least pay me my money, will you?"

"Look, sister, if you can't tell, I'm busy. I said I'd finish it as soon as I can. Now beat it, will you?"

"You have started it, then? When will you finish it?"

"Maybe never. I don't know. Look, kiddo, Mr. Farber said it was something we could maybe use, and I don't think so. It's a piece of Commie propaganda, far's I'm concerned. If I have time maybe I'll look over the rest of it, for Mr. Farber's sake, just so's I can tell him I did. But not today, not this week, maybe not this month."

He started to walk away and I caught his arm. "But Mr. Farber said you'd pay me. I worked on that book all spring, bought the paper, typed it myself, put in all my time on it. I need my money!"

He jerked away. "Get lost before I have you tossed out!" He turned away once more and I didn't move.

"Where is the manuscript? Give it back to me!"

He whirled about, his face a dull red. "I don't know where it is. When it turns up I'll put it in the mail. Get the hell outa here!" His voice rose and other people were watching us now. He motioned to one of the young men in the office. "Throw her out."

The walk home keeps merging in my mind with my horror dream of walking the empty street, and I know that's not how it was, but I can't remember it any other way. At the end of the walk, the huddled mass sitting motionlessly before the building was Jason.

"We were tossed out of our room," he said. "The landlord got a new tenant who signed a year's lease. I thought I'd come over, see how you made out before I started for home."

He had a paper sack with him, his belongings. I sat down on the step by him, and reported.

"You're crying," he said, touching my cheek.

"Don't do that!" I was furious suddenly, at him, at Hanrahan, my mother, the whole stinking world. "Don't touch me!"

"Let's go dancing! Come on, get changed and we'll dance all night!"

"With what?" I had turned away and wouldn't look at him.

"Got a refund of part of our rent. Come on." He pulled me up and pushed me inside the building, up the six flights of stairs.

"What are you doing? Where are you going? When are we going to move?" My mother watched me yank off my clothes and pull on a black skirt and blue blouse, both old, shabby, but the best I had, the clothes I kept for important occasions, like dancing all night with Jason.

"I'll tell you later," I said. "Don't wait up." I dabbed on lipstick, ran the comb through my hair, and ran out to the hallway where Jason was waiting.

We danced in dimly lighted supper clubs and in a large ballroom where a revolving light cast out different colors through red, blue, yellow, green colored glass. We danced in Central Park where shanty town had been, and people threw pennies to a three-piece band playing jazz, and we danced in a speakeasy near the university where we drank bad gin and smoked bad dope. And we danced on the street on our way home at dawn. Jason had become more and more excited throughout the night, and I had caught his excitement. We laughed and giggled and danced like children at a party, and didn't know we were ready to faint from exhaustion.

"I want to dance out of this life to somewhere else!" Jason shouted once, and I wanted that too. It was frenetic, wild, crazy, and we both knew it and yielded to the craziness out of despair. Be crazy or . . . or nothing.

We danced up the stairs to my apartment and I threw the pillows off the sofa for him to sleep on on the floor, and I felt myself falling, falling. He sat on the floor smiling at me. "This has been the happiest time of my life," he said.

"Emily!" I tried not to hear the voice, but it came again, "Emily!" My mother stood in the doorway to her room, her face tight with shock and anger.

Jason sat crosslegged on the floor where I had last seen

him, staring at me. The pillows were as I had thrown them. A flood of terror snapped me wide awake.

"Jason? What's wrong?" He didn't move.

"Emily, what is the meaning of this? I won't live like this! I would rather see you dead and in your grave than living like this!"

"Mother, shut up! Jason, look at me." I touched his hand. He didn't move, didn't even blink. There was the smell of urine. The floor was wet.

"Jason, please! Look at me!" I touched his cheek. It was hot, feverish. He stared straight ahead.

"He's drunk! You went out and got drunk, both of you! You're living a whore's life and I won't tolerate it! You hear me?"

"Shut your goddamn mouth! Get out of here and call a doctor!"

I heard a door slam. She had gone back into her room. I was afraid to leave him, but I had to have help, and finally I went. The doctor I called said I should call Bellevue, that no private doctor would treat anyone in Jason's condition.

I sat on the floor by him, holding his hand until they came and two men got him to his feet and led him away. He walked almost naturally.

"I'm leaving," my mother said after they had gone. "I'm going to Randolf's."

"How will you get there?" I didn't even look at her.

"I have enough money for that," she said. Her voice was self-righteous, indignant, accusatory, hateful.

"You have money?"

I turned then and stared at her in disbelief. She was dressed to go out, hat, coat, gloves, her suitcase at her side. "You have enough money to travel to California?"

"I had a little and Randolf's been sending me money, when he could. I told him you lived like . . . worse than a nigger, and he sent me money so I wouldn't have to do without."

"You have money?" I snatched her purse from her and emptied it on the table. There were bills and silver. I counted. Four hundred dollars, ninety-nine cents. There were three checks for twenty-five dollars each. I began to laugh then.

"I can't see the humor," my mother said. She began to put her things back in her purse. "There was no reason to throw good money after bad. You and that man can blow money on drink, no reason for me to let you use Randolf's hard-earned money. He works hard, tries to live a decent life. . . ."

I'm not even certain now that she said any of that. But she might have. I was laughing too hard to hear what she actually said. The phantom lover strikes again, I thought. For the second time in my life I was being deserted because of a man I had not slept with.

8

There are ghosts in the house. My grandfather walks the halls, searching, still searching. His wife, homesick, as everbearing as a tea rose, hating the man who impregnated her with a regularity that finally must have become shameful to her, prowls the halls after dark, also searching. Perhaps they search for the selves they were when they came to California, the selves that were the first casualties of gold fever, which, like alcoholism, afflicts a few directly, many, many more peripherally. When I was a child there were rumors, told to Randolf by his friends, passed on to Wanda and me, that our grandfather had buried gold in the cellar, or had hidden it somewhere in the house. and that was why our father had been determined to buy it back, in order to search for it. I suppose my buying the house really put the stamp of truth on the rumors.

Father laughed at the talk. His ghost wanders also. Many times I have almost seen it, almost heard it, almost felt it. I have gone into an empty room, felt reluctant to turn on a light for a second or two, as if to allow it time to fade away before it was caught. I never felt that it was Mother, or the grandparents I didn't know. It was Father, never frightening, never chilling the air or doing any of the nonsensical things other peoples' ghosts are said to do. He was just there where he belonged, and at those times I was the intruder, politely waiting a decent interval in order not to interrupt him.

Losing the house killed him. He saw it coming, and permitted himself the luxury of escape through a heart attack. Better to die than to give up. For him the two were not synonymous.

Somehow I can see through this darkness, see myself, my ghost enter the television room to find Scotty at the window, his chin in his hands, not aware of my presence until I speak.

"Look," he says. "You see where the fog starts, down by the curve in the road? You could keep walking straight out on it."

My heart beats strangely. My words, have they been hanging in the air all these years, waiting for him to come along, pick them up, breathe life into them again?

"You could run down the road, throw yourself onto the fog and do a belly flop clear across the bay," I say, as child and adult.

I kneel by him, put my arm across his shoulders.

"You could roll it up and build a fog-man," he says, going beyond the ghost words.

"Roll yourself up in it and hide, come out miles away, like a worm creeping through garden soil."

He screws up his face, thinking, then says, "You could mix chocolate with it and have chocolate fog shakes."

We laugh, and then, still looking out the window, he says, "A kid in my class said San Francisco is going to be shaken loose from the rest of the country and sunk by an earthquake."

"Did he? How does he know that?"

"His dad told him. They're moving to Chicago. His father is a 'lectrician."

"Well, that gives him a certain authority," I say, "but not in geology."

"Are we going to have an earthquake? What's one like?"

"I don't know if we will or not. No one knows for sure. The ground shakes and things rattle. Sometimes buildings get shaken down."

"Why did we come here?"

"Don't you like it here, Scotty? I thought you did."

"Sure I like it, but why are we here if there's going to be an earthquake?"

"Because it's home."

"That's stupid," he says, after a moment to consider it.

"Maybe it is. There are things that can hurt you everywhere. Hurricanes, volcanoes, tornadoes, floods, lightning, piranha fish. You really have to watch out for those piranhas. They're looking for you all the time." I dig my fingers into his sides, tickling him, and he falls down to the window seat in helpless laughter. "What piranhas love more than anything in the world," I say, snapping my teeth close to his ear, "are little boys' pink ears."

He shrieks and tries to cover his ears and protect his sides, and we roll to the floor, playing, laughing.

Scotty's ghost walks the house, and he isn't even dead. I catch a glimpse of him now and again, playing with miniature cars under the kitchen table, sliding down the banister to land on cushions on the floor in the living room, digging up the cellar—he heard the rumor about gold and dug a swimming-pool-sized hole in the far end where the furnace is and the floor is packed dirt.

We were awed by the hole, he no less than I. We stood side by side, with Dorrie behind us, scolding, and I kept thinking, he's so small to dig such a large hole. It took him three days to fill it in again. I look up from work sometimes to listen for his voice, certain that a moment earlier he called.

At the window, with the fog lifting, I think of Scotty's question—Why are we here? How the sea fog gentles the city. My father and my grandfather both sat here in this place and gazed across the bay at Sausalito and Belvedere and beyond to Mount Tamalpais, all softened to a pastel gray-green that is like the coloring of some fairy-tale illustration, but more so than the artist could capture. When my grandfather built, this was the highest hill in the city, and from here my father looked down on the Hopkins Mansion on Nob Hill, farther down to Telegraph Hill, down to the harbor, where the voices of fog horns mingled without pause. Over there, Chinatown, complete with tiny pagodas and opium dens, cribs, and factories, a city within the city, unplanned, unknown to the white community, its maze of streets, alleys, and passages defied laws and common sense. Worse was the filled land at the edge of the sea where men dumped their refuse to create earth from water and on it erected warehouses, hotels, flimsy buildings that often slipped and fell, only to be rebuilt with their own timbers. From here my father watched it burn.

From here, with the magic of the sea fog's pale filter to blend all edges into air, to halo every light, the city was then and is now of incomparable beauty.

We tell ourselves it wasn't the earthquake that was so deadly, it was the fire, as if the city would have burned if the water mains had not been ruptured and the fire-alarm system not wrecked, and the gas lines not broken. This is what we tell ourselves, and we lie.

After you discount those who are too conservative to move, or too ignorant, or too assured of personal salvation, or too fatalistic or optimistic, those who gamble with time—planning to stay long enough to finish this or that, to make a killing in the real-estate market, or some other way—after all these are tabulated, there is left over a group, no one knows how large or small, that also stays, and it is this group, of which I am one, that bears investigation. Another article note, except there will be no more articles. . . .

Tony wants to take me to his home in Napa Valley, the same valley my father and his brother trudged through on their trek to find a fortune. Tony's house is as large as mine, and in excellent repair, with a coterie of servants to keep it so. There are grapes, and a winery, not very large, but with the highest reputation for good wine. Tony is always very nervous when he comes to the Bay Area, which he does several times a month.

"Why me, Tony? There must be dozens of younger women who would move in tomorrow?"

"I don't want them. I want a woman I can talk to, someone who has read a book or two, who knows the difference between Leibnitz and Listerine."

"There are many intelligent, educated women. Again, why me? I'm not young, older than you are, in fact, and God knows I'm not good-looking."

"I don't want a young good-looking intelligent woman. I want you, and God alone knows why, but I do."

"Tony, stop before you say something I'll regret. You're a very dear person, you know. But I won't marry you and move out into the country. I have my work here. You like to pick grapes and stamp on them or whatever it is you do to them, and I love my work. They wouldn't mix, darling. They wouldn't."

"You could fly over here anytime you wanted to. I'm not asking you to stop working, but you'll have to one of these years and then what will you do?"

"I'll never stop working. Not really. Any more than you will. Now can we go out for dinner? I'm famished."

"Emily, it isn't the country, not like you make it sound. And I don't stamp the goddamn grapes. Just don't say no right now. Let it simmer first. Why did you put me off until tonight? What were you doing Wednesday?"

"Kenneth had a show. It was a smashing success, and afterward there was a champagne party. . . ."

"You went with him?"

"Yes, certainly. And I threw the party. You should have come to town for it. I'm sorry you didn't."

"You know I won't go to things like that. Is he another lover?"

"Don't get sulky, it's not becoming."

"Is he? Isn't he staying with you at Hotel Deadbeat?"

"Tony, you sound like a jealous schoolboy."

"That's how I feel. I can see them looking at me at the airport, the smirks on their faces. They know there's a woman. And riding over here, my heart starts twitching, and I begin to worry, maybe you won't make it after all, maybe you're tied up, on your way to New York, having a champagne party for one of your protégés. Maybe you've found someone else you like better. My God, Emily, no one's done this to me since I was seventeen, and I don't like it!"

"Then stop coming here."

"Oh, Christ." He turned over and put his face against my breast and said again, softly, "Oh, Christ."

"What it is, I think, is that he finds it somehow humiliating to be having an affair with a woman who is nearly seventy, who has white hair and wears glasses on a black silk ribbon, and who can't sew a hem.

"You'll stay here and get yourself killed in the next earthquake," he said once, nervous because the ground had shifted a bit only moments before. Not much, not enough to rattle the windows even, but enough to make one pause and wait, and to count . . . I hippopotamus, 2 hippopotamus . . .

"One way or another, sooner or later, what we all have in common is the same future."

"But you don't have to go looking for it! It'll come soon enough without that."

"You're afraid of dying, aren't you, Tony? What a strange thing to contemplate about you."

"Everyone is afraid of dying. Some hide it better than others."

I shook my head. "I'm not afraid. Not really. I'm afraid of suffering, of being incapable, of being bedridden or hospitalized with machinery plugged into me keeping me legally alive."

"I don't believe you."

"I don't care."

"That's the trouble with you, Emily Carmichael! You don't care what anyone else thinks. You're too wrapped in your own life, your own selfish life, to care about anyone else."

His wife had been one year younger than he and she had died, and now he wanted a wife who was older than he, someone who had defied death at fifty-six, who has lived more years than he has, proving that death could be postponed. Knowing why he wants to marry me, or one of the reasons, does not mean that I doubt him when he says he loves me. I think Tony loves me deeply and would make a very good husband, if only I wanted to marry.

He drew up papers taking care of me forever after we married. He showed them to me, signed, notarized, witnessed, needing only a wedding ceremony to activate the various clauses. I could keep up the handouts, he said, and even pay Dorrie a bigger salary than I had in the past. She could be my personal maid, or companion, whatever I wanted. I could keep up Hotel Deadbeat and let the kids hang out there, if that would make me happy. My money would be mine without any questions or strings attached.

"I'm a damn lonely man, Emily. I've found myself thinking it would be better to marry someone off the streets than to go on living alone, and that scared me, really scared me."

Scotty hates him, but then Scotty hates every man I've ever talked to—Maury, Louis, Kenneth, even poor old Colonel McGowan. I think he hates Tony the most, possibly because, like Tony, he is humiliated by the thought that his mother, nearly seventy, could be having an affair with a very wealthy man who is five years younger than she.

Tony's wife died eight years ago, two years before I met him. His three children are married, gone. He is like a man who hungers for a meal that is safely locked up behind a clear strong pane of glass, forever out of reach. His marriage had been happy, he said, and of course that would make it worse for him. He really should have married again almost immediately. He says I am nothing like his wife.

He couldn't believe it when I turned him down the night he proposed five years ago. He could believe it even less when I suggested he come visit me at home, stay the weekend. The following week he bought the condominium—two bedrooms, on the fourteenth floor, overlooking the sea. He came to my house one time only, I visited him at his house one time only. We meet regularly in the two-bedroom condominium, which neither of us likes. Sometimes he cooks dinner for us. I never offer to. I am as bad a cook as I am a seamstress.

"You are skinny," he said, early, still smarting from my refusal. "You are homely, your nose is too long, and you could fix your hair if you would."

"So why am I here? Why are you here with me?" We were side by side on the king-size bed, the windows open to the sea breeze, which was fast turning into a gale, so chilling the room that we huddled under the blankets, neither of us willing to leave the warmth long enough to get up and close the windows.

"I lie awake at night and ask myself that very question," he said. "The only answer I come up with is that I must be crazy."

"It's because I like you," I said, shivering, snuggling closer to him, determined not to be the one to get up and close the windows. "I like you, respect you, and refuse to be dependent on you for anything." Anything more lasting than the brief chill of closing the window.

"Just 'like'?" He was stiff and angry with me.

"It's a lot harder to find someone you can like than someone to love. And best to have both because if love dies, as it often does, you know, you don't have to shed the other person like a molting snake sheds its skin."

After a moment he sighed deeply, threw back the covers, got up and closed the windows.

"If I could just understand why," he said once. "You are always worried about money, and you have to escape to the beach cottage just to find quiet. You live in a madhouse and you know it. Why?"

I couldn't make him understand. "There are diamonds to be cut," I said lightly. "And I have the tools. That's all."

"It isn't as if no one else could do what you do."

"What a pity you've always been so rich you've never had to learn to be diplomatic."

"What the hell does that mean?"

"If I were a Rembrandt, or a Chopin, or a Shakespeare, or you name it, any real artist or genius, then you could understand why I have to do my work. But I'm only a run-of-the-mill editor, and I could resign tomorrow and never be missed."

"I didn't say that."

"But you did. And it's a valid point, but it isn't valid in this instance. The life you'd prescribe for me would be lovely for almost any woman alive, but not me. What would I do all day every day? After I helped you stamp the grapes and cork the bottles, then what?"

"We'd find things, Emily. Believe me, there are things. We would travel, entertain, meet fascinating people, shop in Hong Kong, look at pyramids in Egypt. . . ."

"Go find interesting things," I said, and patted him on the cheek, "but, my darling, I don't have to move a foot to have things interesting right now. You know when I'm happiest? It's when I am fighting against a deadline, when I know I have a brilliant article, or the best art that any magazine has run in years, or an exciting new poet to publish; it's when one of my unknowns blooms before my eyes into a respected writer or photographer; it's when I sit down with the first copy of the new issue and read it with a stranger's eyes and marvel at how well it all goes together, at the scope and the beauty of the writing or the pictures. Someone else could edit, sure, but no one else would have put together that particular issue."

I was speaking a foreign language to him, not one word of which was intelligible. A few weeks later he handed me a box that held a necklace of emeralds and diamonds. I gasped when I saw it.

"It suits you," he said. "You should wear emeralds."

I held it up and looked at my reflection in the mirror,

saw with disappointment that the reflection was shaking its head.

"What do you mean?" he demanded.

"It's beautiful. I can't keep it."

"What's that supposed to mean? I'm giving it to you."

I shook my head and held the necklace out toward him. "I can't."

"You mean it's your policy not to accept jewelry from your lovers?" His voice was bitter and hateful.

"No one ever tried me on emeralds and diamonds before," I said. "I'm as sorry as you to learn I can't keep it. I think it's a disgusting trait to find lurking in myself."

"It would give me pleasure to see you wear it and look beautiful for it."

"I'm not a tree you can decorate! And I'm not a whore you can pay off. What would give you pleasure would be shameful to me. I won't have it."

The necklace dangled between us, swinging, flashing with each movement. He made no motion to take it and I opened my fingers and let it fall to the floor, heavily carpeted, it is true, but the gesture was understood.

"You're a fool! You're a selfish, conceited, stupid fool! That necklace cost more than you make in several years."

"And you're a miserable rich bastard who thinks he can buy what isn't on the market! I said I won't be dependent on you! I will not!"

He glared and I glared back until the very ludicrousness of the situation forced me to giggle, then to laugh and turn away. A moment later he was laughing also.

"I am crazy," he said. "I'm sorry."

I laughed even harder. And he held me and we laughed together, no longer certain why, only that something had happened, as if we had been stalled at a fog-shrouded crossroads, and had stumbled and groped our way past it into a better, cleaner place. Later he bought me a thin gold chain with a jointed gold fish on it, and I wear it with pleasure. The fish signifies long life and good luck, I think.

Tony has heard about the earthquake by now surely. Perhaps he can not charter a flight up here; aircraft are grounded, or the fields are destroyed. Or he has gone to the house, not knowing I am here at the beach. He is digging through the rubble, calling my name. Perhaps he'll find the buried gold and hold it for me. He could hide it, afraid that the new independence it would provide would forever keep us apart. At one hundred forty-two dollars an ounce, a valise of say twenty pounds would be . . . ? I need a calculator. I always lose the decimal, and zeroes are tricky, appearing and vanishing at random. Say forty-five thousand. Not enough. That is what is frightening. I can't lose my job and steady income, there is no way I can keep the house without it. My pension will support me, I suppose, but given the choice of living in a tiny apartment with no work, no seminars going on in the living room, no dance rehearsals in the television room, no darkroom activities below, no twins plotting against their warring parents, no library tables spread with pictures, bits of text, advertisements, with Red and Constance there fighting over space, I can understand in a way never before possible why retired people often choose a heart attack over the available alternatives. Maybe the valise is a footlocker, with a hundred pounds, or five hundred!

I'll have to give up this cottage. This was to be my last trip out here, except for the final one with Dorrie to pack up. I tried to buy the cottage a few years ago, but Mr. Rossiter wouldn't sell.

"I'd be nuts to sell any of them," he said frankly. "I built them, six in all, did everything myself, even the plumbing. Good job I did of it too. Snug, warm, pretty. Make two thousand on a yearly lease on each one of them. Sell and I'd be out capital gains tax, and income. Be nuts."

There is a large L-shaped living room with a fireplace spacious enough to accommodate the immense driftwood logs that are there for the taking on the beach. There are two upper bedrooms with fireplaces, baths and closets. The kitchen is very modern, it opens to a wide porch. Over the porch there is a balcony the width of the house, accessible from the bedrooms. There is an attached garage on the kitchen side.

I keep thinking that by daylight someone will notice that my cottage has fallen down, but I know that that is as pointless as trying to figure how much money five hundred pounds of gold is worth. The cliffs the cottage sat on make a plateau here, with room enough for the house and driveway, then they rise another hundred feet and up there, back two hundred yards, are three more of Mr. Rossiter's cottages, but no one is in them at this time of year. My cottage is easily visible from the sea. A fisherman will notice, or the Coast Guard, or a tramp steamer, or a herd of gray whales. . . .

How Dorrie hates it out here. The sound of the surf makes her nervous, she lies awake waiting for the next wave to thunder onto the beach. And she begins to sneeze as soon as she smells the beach.

Scotty and I used to spend weekends here, until he was fourteen, when he became a stranger to me. Suddenly he had to accept a fact that his reality had never demanded he see before, and reality shifted for him. He was overwhelmed by the new truth.

"Generations were traumatized when they had to admit finally that the earth is not the center of the universe," my father said. "They had evidence that the earth was the center, that God made the heavens revolve around the earth, and it all vanished overnight—worthless, false evidence. In a twinkling the universe became something altogether different, the facts added up to different truths that made possible new theories about creation, about astronomy, geology, everything."

In a twinkling Scotty's truths became worthless and his reality had to admit other truths. In that twinkling he became a stranger. There were nearly fourteen good years, and since then twenty years with an occasional good moment. If I weep, it will be for Scotty and me. There is so much to finish, to be put right.

Scotty, though he dances on the ocean floor and celebrates the creation of earth, must eventually return to the house, to my side, and at that time he will have to accept me and examine whatever truths he has assembled. Until he does, he will continue to run away and hide from human contacts, he will be cold and proper and unhappy; marry and divorce as often as he will, there will be no peace, no acceptance of another, until he can accept me and then himself.

"Emily, you really are not fair. You insist on being exactly what you want, and forcing people to alter their own concepts of right and wrong, proper and improper."

"Maury! You here? Hold my hand, will you? I think I am getting frightened."

"You are avoiding the issue, as usual. Whenever you are wrong, you change the subject, and presently I have forgotten myself what the issue was."

"I don't force anyone to anything. Never!"

"But you do. You make no concessions at all to customs, to mores. You are an anarchist, you live in a world without standards, and few others can function in such a world."

"All my life people have told me, you must do this, you must learn that or you will be an old maid, you won't have children at your feet, you will be lonely, you will be an outcast. Think this, behave like that. What they have told me most is that I must be married, have a man to take care of me, to give Scotty a name. I gave him a name, a fine name, and I have taken care of myself. What is so bad about that? Why am I suspect because I can take care of myself?"

"Because you threaten the system and if the system fails, civilization collapses."

"*I* threaten the collapse of civilization?" This makes me laugh again, and when I am done there is only the sound of the surf. For a moment I think, All I have to do is repent, say I am sorry, and a miracle will happen. The house will right itself, the chaise will return to the wall position, my bed will be secure; and I will awaken from a vivid dream, a nightmare that ends with dawn. That requires faith, not facts that say it cannot happen. With faith enough it could happen. But would a nonbeliever see it happen? And that is the crux, that is why faith has eluded me—I would be one of the faithful, and also, I would be the observer measuring effects with yardsticks and thermometers.

9

I dreamed I was dancing at a party at Leslie Tobias's house in London. Leslie gave lovely parties. There was a wide empty room that he never furnished at all and we danced to Glenn Miller and Cab Calloway and Benny Goodman records all night. Leslie collected Americans. He was killed during the blitz. He called me Emilidarlin.

"Are you sleeping with him?" Maury demanded, holding me too tightly, paying no attention to the music, or to the others in the room.

"No. But it's hardly any of your business, is it?"

"It's my business. Let's get the hell out of here."

"Maury, aren't you happy to see me? When Leslie said you were coming here tonight, I thought what a surprise I'd be for you. I thought you would be pleased, but you've scowled and scolded and muttered until I wonder if I shouldn't simply go back to my flat and pretend I don't know you're in town."

"Come on." He yanked my arm and pulled me from the room, from the house. Leslie Tobias waved as we passed him. On the sidewalk before the house Maury stopped and kissed me fiercely. "I didn't know you were going to be there. What the devil are you doing in London?"

"Working. What are you doing in London?"

"I'm on government business." He shook his head. "I thought I had lost my mind when I saw you there."

"You'll be here for the holidays?"

"Do you share your apartment with anyone?"

"No."

He hailed a cab and we went home. We made love and then lay side by side talking until dawn, when we made love again.

"You can't stay here," he said. "It's crazy, your being here at this time."

"You're here."

"But I'm leaving next week. Emily, I love you. Come home with me now. We'll work something out."

"A mistress in an out-of-the-way apartment, waiting for you to have a free evening? Is that how you'll work it out?"

"You could get a good job with the government now. I know enough people to arrange that, for Christ sake! We could see each other."

"Maury, not now. Don't ask me like this. Not because you're frightened and lonely and your marriage hasn't worked as it should. You're tired and discouraged and I wouldn't be able to change any of that. Now you can forget it when we're together, but that wouldn't last, and the fatigue and discouragement would catch up wherever we happened to be."

"I love you. I want you to be near."

"No, Maury. You just happened to run into me here. If I were in Antarctica and you came charging down there behind a dog sled, mushing all the way, then I'd believe you really were out hunting for me. But here? You just happened to come upon me. Darling, I'd be number three on your list of priorities! And I couldn't bear that. I'm too egotistical to bear that."

"If I can line up a good job for you, will you take it? No strings. Just a good job with a future."

I shook my head, smiling at him, even loving him. "I don't want to work in Washington for the government. I don't believe in government. I don't like bureaucracies. I want to do editorial work, maybe for a book publisher after this is over. Maybe with a magazine, I'm not sure. But I am very sure of what I don't want." I waved toward the city. "Besides, I have a job here, remember. No one's told me I'll be fired next week. As long as it lasts, I'll stick with it."

"That won't be long. Emily, Hitler is going to overrun all of Europe, and then he'll be ready to tackle England. We don't know how long it's going to take to prepare England to resist, maybe there won't be enough time. You have to get out of here."

"Are we going to get in the war?"

"No! FDR has promised we will stay out of it."

Politics, I thought, just as my mother before me must have thought when they talked about the judge.

"Aren't you satisfied, Maury? You were so enthusiastic before. What happened?"

He lighted a cigarette and took a long time answering. "I don't even know. Everything is slower than we thought it would be. There's a lot of discontent back home, still a lot of problems that seem insoluble. Our analysts say things are developing in an orderly fashion, but I don't know. Jason is afraid it's going to take a war economy to pull the country back together again. I just don't know. There's hardly time enough to think about next week much less next year or the five years ahead."

"Jason? Jason Mohr? You're in touch with Jason?"

"He's on the staff. Didn't you know? He was ill for a while, then he came to Washington and we had a talk. He was sorry his book failed in the reworking of the material, but we all know that happens sometimes. . . ."

"What do you mean, it failed?"

"I never saw it. Jason said that after he recovered, he read the manuscript with enough distance to be able to judge it and it was a failure. Of course, in light of the success of Keynes's theories, there's little point in duplicating the effort." He looked at me closely. "What's wrong?"

"It was a brilliant book, a brilliant analysis, brilliant reasoning, and by the time we were finished with it, it was readable. It wasn't a failure."

He shifted uncomfortably. "Well, it's his, and his opinion is the one that matters, I suppose. After all, you said you knew nothing of politics and finances."

"Not until I read that book. Where is Jason now? Washington?"

"He's here, in London. Are you sure about his book, Emily? Hanrahan agreed that it was a failure."

"That bastard owes me five hundred dollars," I muttered.

Maury looked shaken. "He didn't pay you?" I shook my head. "I'll pay you."

"Not you. Hanrahan."

"It won't matter to him. He's an ugly cheap little politician. The woods are full of Hanrahans, but God help us, we need them. We can't get along without them."

For four days the American staff met with the British staff to work out the details of the pending high-level conference, the details of the agenda only, not the actual agreements, he said glumly. "You have to plan what you'll talk about, how you'll approach the issue, who will participate, make certain a counterpart from the other side is present, and this, mind you, among friends!"

Maury was overworked and depressed. Estelle was unhappy, he was unhappy, they both loved without restraint their three-year-old daughter, who was severely retarded; she and old loyalties, debts that could never be repaid, made a curious bond, as if to cement with misery that which could not be held together with love. But it was more than this that weighed him down. I knew there was more without knowing what it was. Maury had heard a devil whispering in his ear; although he had managed not to hear the words yet, he lived in dread of the day when they would become coherent.

On the fifth day Jason showed up at my door. Mr. Farber, he said, had been called home, and had gotten a ride on a government plane that hadn't allowed him time to say goodbye, and could he come in please, and how are you Emily?

Jason, unlike Maury, was happy. "It's okay to talk about that day, if you want," he said right away. "Thank you for trying to get in to see me and for writing. I'm sorry I never answered. There seemed little point to it then, and later I felt I'd be intruding, and a little silly."

"You look marvelous! And prosperous!"

"Yes. They pay well enough. I'm one of those bright young men you read about in the papers and magazines these days. We plan to save the world." He laughed, and I felt a touch of uneasiness.

He was not quite as thin as before; his clothes were good and they fitted him, and his hands remained quiet now where before they had gesticulated wildly. He had

had his teeth fixed. And he looked at me directly, so long and so directly that I turned away.

"Why did you tell Maury your book was bad? You know that's a lie."

"The book was a lie. It was heresy. We worship at the altar of the great god Keynes now and the old gods are banished to the nether lands. We no longer speak their names."

"You sold out."

"I was converted. The road to Damascus was by way of Washington, where I saw the light. I wanted to ride a white horse and save the world all by myself, and now I know only teamwork will lead to salvation, and deficit financing." He smiled a wide, ingenuous smile. His smile was brightened with gold. "Let's have dinner together."

"You weren't like that!" I cried. "You were a bird soaring above everything, with incredible vision that saw what few others could suspect even existed."

"A bird in the bush is worth a hand," he said, laughing. "I'm hungry. Come on. One of the things they taught me in the hospital is the value of regular meals."

Through dinner he talked furiously of the things he had seen in London, of the impossibility of bypassing the bureaucracy to get anything done in the government, of the beautiful Indian girl he worshiped from a distance, of his father, who was crazy. And through it all he continued to smile.

"My mother is crazy, too," I said.

He nodded. "She has her little fantasy world that is nicer than this world. I don't blame her for staying in it."

"She isn't happy."

"Not in this world. But what about when she is in the one she invented? When she sits doing nothing for hours? Who can say if she is happy or not then?"

I shivered. "Are you well now, Jason? You are so different."

For a moment the smile froze, then he relaxed and laughed. "Tell you a story," he said, leaning across the table toward me, lowering his voice. "This slob in the hospital, just a guy, a nobody. They caught him on the Brooklyn Bridge, naked as a baby, getting ready to jump. There were things he wanted to think about before he did it, you see. That's how it is sometimes. They hauled him in, drugs, the routine, kept him quiet a couple of weeks.

When they took him off the dope, he tried to bite his way through his wrist, gnawed away real good. More drugs, more everything they do there. He tried again and they did a lobotomy. He came out smiling a lot and didn't have much to say, but one day he tried it another time. They hadn't cut deeply enough, I guess. They didn't get the devil, and they went back in and scraped awhile, cut a bit deeper, you know. Snickersnee with the little ol' scalpel, and that damn cunning devil evaded the blade again. The next time they brought him back without his teeth." Jason sat back in his chair, smiling widely. He drank his wine, poured more, still smiling. "You're staring. You didn't like my story."

"It's hideous. It's atrocious! How long were you there?"

"Nine months. Then I was delivered of a ten-ton psychosis and the afterbirth was a clutch of neuroses. They should have let him have his way on the bridge," he said calmly. "Or they should have tried once and then let him have pills, to take or not. His choice. When they realized they couldn't see what he saw and couldn't make him stop seeing it, they should have butted out. Now he sees it day in, day out, and will for the rest of his life. They point to him with pride. He's one they saved."

"But they have to try to help people. They do cure some people. They cured you. You're doing worthwhile work, you're content, aren't you?"

His smile froze again, and I closed my eyes, chilled and frightened. His voice was low when he spoke. "What you do, the cure, is simply not tell them what they don't want to hear. You don't upset their world view and they are delighted with you and pat you on the head and let you go." He laughed and touched my cheek. "It's all right. I learned something. You can stop, you see, and just let the world take over, or you don't have to. It was pleasant to stop, and all the time I knew I could get up, I could start again, but I didn't want to, didn't care. I know that now and don't have to learn it again. It's all right."

"But you don't believe in what you're doing, not like Maury."

"Mr. Farber is walking on the coals, and I'm on the sideline wondering if he'll wake up while he's still on them or after he gets off at the end. I'm afraid he's going to blister his soul."

"Why? FDR is doing more than anyone thought he could."

He laughed again and stood up. "Let's go dancing. FDR," he said, counting money for the tip, "is living a miracle. He's feeding loaves to the multitude of fish."

The next day I shopped for a present for him. It was Christmas Eve. I bought a small malachite globe paperweight that was intricately carved with a map of the world. It looked much like the earth from space as it was to appear in two decades; the artist was truly gifted with prescience. When I got to my apartment, Jason was pacing before the building, there was a basket on the steps, and a tiny Christmas tree leaned against the rail.

He had brought cold roast chicken, champagne, a can of pears, cheese, decorations for the tree, and a package wrapped in red tissue paper.

We decorated the tree, ate, and then danced to radio music by candlelight. At midnight we could exchange presents, Jason said, not before. At eleven an announcer came on with late news and Jason turned the radio off.

"Let's go to church," he said. "Come on."

"But . . . I don't even know where a church is."

"I do. I passed one coming over this evening. About four blocks away. I haven't been to church on Christmas Eve in fifteen years."

The church was tiny, almost hidden by cypress trees. Around the property was a wall with a stone archway. Later, it was bombed to rubble. I stood in the street the day after it was destroyed, remembering.

"It says there," Jason said, pointing to a bronze plate, "this church was built in 1595." The building was gray with blacked-out slit windows above stained-glass medieval scenes. From inside, the slit windows turned out to be pale yellow glass with a burning candle in each of them. I wondered how they were lighted, so high up. The church was filled, and the choir was in the middle of a Bach cantata when we sat down in the rear.

The music soared, first the organ, then the voices answering, the organ again, together swelling triumphantly, filling the church, expanding the church until it was the world, and the world was filled with glorious music. A soprano's voice rose, climbed higher effortlessly, then higher still and I felt the voice inside my head and rose with it. I

was hardly aware when the music stopped, and there was
the drone of a minister's voice instead.

Jason took my arm and said, not in a whisper, "Let's
get out of here. They never leave well enough alone."

Outside, the night air felt cold on my cheeks and I realized I had been weeping. I wiped my face.

"You were crying like a baby," Jason said roughly.
"What were you thinking?"

I shook my head. I hadn't been thinking anything at all.

"Experiencing, then," he said.

"I don't know. Flying, rising in the air and plummeting,
but under control, rising again . . ." I shook my head
again. That wasn't it. "I don't know."

He walked fast, his hand hard on my arm. "The music
released the church from the drabness of every day," he
said. "It let it be the numinous place it was meant to be.
You could feel . . . feel power, the power expressed there
down the centuries, through music. Why can't they know
that? Why can't they let it go at that? Not try to explain,
not try to use reason to define an experience that is beyond reason?"

Inside my apartment again he still paced, too restless
now to be stilled, and the old Jason was back, the Jason I
had known in the Twelfth Street tenement.

"You almost lose yourself," he said. "You can feel the
self slipping out, almost finding someplace else, someplace
grand and beautiful and with hope, and then an ass starts
braying and you are jerked back."

"Jason, stop. Please. Look at your present. Tell me if
you like it. Let me see what's in my box?"

"It isn't from me," he said. "It's from him. He had it
ready for you, then his wife called. The kid has
pneumonia or something. He asked me to deliver it." He
got the red tissue-wrapped box from the little tree and
handed it to me. I held it a moment, then put it down on
the table.

"Open yours," I said.

"Here's a little something I picked up for you." Jason
said then, and reached into his overcoat pocket and
brought out a narrow box. It wasn't wrapped.

It was a gold pencil with my name on it.

"I kept thinking how many pencils you wore out on my
book," Jason said. "Is it all right?"

"It's the best present I've ever had." The pencil is on my

desk next to the worn agate. The name engraved on it is almost illegible now. "Open yours."

Suddenly he laughed. "My God," he said, "you've given me the world!"

He swept me up and around and we both laughed and thanked each other at once, and then he kissed me. Someone had taught him how to kiss.

"Can I make love to you?" he asked, drawing back, looking at me intently. "I've wanted to for years, you know."

"I didn't know."

"Oh, yes. I used to walk you all over New York instead. And danced you all night instead. It wasn't the same, though."

Behind me on the table lay the red box, and back home Maury was with his wife and child, and here was this intense man whose eyes were piercing, who wept with me at church, and railed at the minister for breaking the spell, and I thought in wonder, It's been him for all these years. It's been Jason all these years! My mother had seen what I couldn't see at the time; essentially she had been right. Her timing was wrong, that was all.

I woke up near dawn and groped for him, but he was not there, and gradually my eyes adjusted and I saw him standing at the window. He was naked.

"You'll get chilled," I said, going to him. He was shivering. His skin was like that of a dead person.

"I thought I heard bombers," he said, his teeth chattering. "A nightmare. Bombers here! They'll come, Emily. The war will come here."

"Come to bed. You're so cold."

"I dreamed they were already here." He didn't move from the window. I dragged the blanket off the bed and took it to him, wrapped us both in it and stood by him, staring at the dark city.

"Sometimes at night, never in the day, I get frightened," he said softly, still rigid. "I think about that day and wonder if I'm kidding myself that I could have got up, could have done anything. We had a psych teacher who demonstrated hypnosis for the class. The subjects all said later they didn't have to do what he told them, but they wanted to, or at least they didn't want not to. I always wondered, they really wanted to bark like dogs, or crow like roosters, or get stuck with pins? I didn't believe it. I don't believe it, and yet . . . somehow I do believe it. It's pleasant to let someone else take charge, you know? Just give up and let someone else run you, run everything. And I get afraid all over again."

"Jason, you were pushing yourself too hard. Not enough sleep, not enough to eat, working day and night, worrying . . . That's over now."

"The devil's still in me, Emily. I pretended it was gone. When they said it was fatigue, I agreed and slept day and night for a while. When they said it was malnutrition, I had second helpings of everything. But I knew I was pretending. I knew it was still in me. I was afraid they would pull my teeth. When I began getting paychecks, the first thing I did was go to the dentist. I don't want them to pull my teeth."

"I'll make us some tea," I said desperately. "Come sit down. You're so cold." I pulled his arm and he moved with me to the table and sat down. He smiled at me then.

"It was the nightmare," he said. "I'm sorry. I hate nightmares. They weaken you, you're in no shape to deny anything, you just accept the terror no matter how impossible it is, no matter that you could destroy it just by opening your eyes, you simply accept it and submit to it."

"You said once, when we were working, that you just wanted to wake up a dozen people, remember?" I had the tea kettle on, spooned tea into the pot.

"But I didn't do it. I didn't wake up anyone, and instead I went to sleep along with the rest, and now and then when I open my eyes I am terrified and want only to go to sleep again."

I sat down and took his hand. "Jason, can't you just live your own life and forget the world? Can't you just be one person living one lifetime? It's too late now to try to save anything. There will be another chance later, but it's too late now."

"The chance was ten years ago, maybe," he said, smiling his strange mirthless smile. "It was already too late when I looked around and started to work on my book. That was too late. We're hypnotized, all of us, already. All over Europe people want to go to war. They want to bomb each other, maim and destroy, torture, kill. . . . Soon we'll want to go to war too. And we'll build bigger and better bombers, kill more and more people than ever. We'll want to because they tell us we want to. And we'll say we want to get killed, to see others get killed, that it's a good, even a holy thing we're doing. And then they'll want us to want to do something else, and we'll nod and say, yes, that's what we want to do. And we'll never wake up again."

The tea kettle began to whistle and he jerked his hand as if he had been touched by the boiling water. Silently I made the tea, put bread, butter, and cheese on the table, and we ate breakfast. Dawn was lightening the sky. It was Christmas Day. Church bells were starting to ring.

No one worked much during the week between Christmas and New Year's. He laughed at the stories I filed. Lies, he said cheerfully. All lies, but it didn't matter. We danced often. He was a marvelous dancer, should have been a professional dancer. When I told him so, he laughed, and told me about his father.

"He's sixty now, stooped, with a bad leg from World War One. He was a farmer, they lost the land and went to New York, where he learned that an unskilled worker takes what he can find. The hat factory. He's a Lutheran, very strict, very much a believer. We all had to go to church and Sunday school when we were kids, no card playing, no profanity, no drinking, nothing but hard work, church, and duty to one's parents and state. I wanted to dance, always did. One day he caught me spinning around in the living room and he walloped me halfway across the room. A boy who dances becomes a homosexual, that was his message of the day. I was confined to quarters for the next month and he watched me like a hawk watches a hatching egg, ready to swoop at the first tottering step. I stiff-legged my way around the apartment for months and months afterward. So, I didn't take up dancing and I was saved. I didn't become a homosexual."

"No, you didn't," I agreed, and we both laughed.

"He's crazy now, of course," Jason said, smiling. "He talks to God and that's not new, he always did. But now God's talking back to him and that's not so good. God puts strange ideas in his head."

Stop! Stop! I don't want to think about Jason. I don't want to live through it again, never again. I want to stop, but our figures dancing, laughing, loving, keep swirling before my eyes. Please stop, I whisper; there is only the surf to hear, and it never listens.

"Emily?"

"Jason! Everyone is coming here. Why not? I am in, receiving callers throughout the night. Jason, you look beautiful!"

"And you are beautiful. You never believed that, did you? Every man who loved you swore it and you never believed any of them."

"Men in love are not the world's great judges of beauty."

"But they are the only ones to judge. They are the only ones who see it. The rest of the world sees only the mask."

"Jason, why? I could have loved you forever. I could have kept you safe. We could have gone somewhere, the two of us, and you would have been safe."

"I knew I couldn't control it, Emily. I kept pretending I could. But I knew if it happened again, next time they would pull my teeth."

"What could you have seen that was that awful? I lived through it, many of us did, and it passed."

"There are some plants that you can cut off and put down in dirt out in the cold, just sticks really, that's all they are, but calluses form where they were cut and when that happens, you can plant them and new roots will grow from the callused ends, new plants will take hold and thrive. You're like them, Emily. But I would have shriveled and died, or rotted and died."

"What did you see?"

"I saw . . ."

"Jason, I can't hear you! Don't go away again, please! Jason, I loved you. I still love you!"

"Emily, didn't you hear? That was the problem then too. I tried and no one heard, no one could hear."

"Jason, don't go away. I'm frightened. I'm so alone and frightened now. Stay with me."

"Remember how you held me when I became frightened and cold," he said. "You were so warm, your arms so firm and strong. I almost stayed with you. For a while I believed your warm strong arms could keep me safe. Is that better?"

I can feel him now, holding me, his voice whispering in my ear, whispering. . . .

10

I am suspended, separated from all motion, all change, in a now that has been extended beyond comprehension. Now is nothing, a void; only the past imperfectly remembered and the future imprecisely visualized are real and one is no less real than the other. Impressions left from memory traces and anticipations, that is now, where we weave strands from the one direction, cast a line into the other, and pull ourselves along it into tomorrow.

How to be selective, not ruled by caprice, ignorance, cupidity, stupidity, serendipity . . . How to explain those who refuse. Jason, so young to have cried out, "No more!" My mother: "I am weary now. I'm not afraid and I am ready to stop. The shadows are gone." Wanda thought she meant the shadow of fear, shadow of death. She meant the shadows of the future: I see them shadows that coalesce and become activated in reveries, in dreams, then sink back to insubstantial figures. When there are no more shadows, then one is ready, one no longer weaves a line to cast into the future. One of the shadows in that future must be myself; sometimes it seems to turn to gaze back at me, to reach out and lay a hand on me that I can feel in a way that no words have been invented to describe. I reached out to myself as child, dancing at the edge of the lava fields, touched the child I was, reassured the child I was. Did I as child sense a shadow from the future? I don't know.

And that's the final frustration: we don't know, we can't be certain; there is no proof.

"My whole life flashed before my eyes." I can accept that. If one steps inadvertently into an extended now where time does not exist, there is time enough to replay a life, a dozen lives, over and over, time to dread, to wish, to hurt, to yearn for, to regret, to find or lose faith. . . .

I suppose I could die here. Perhaps I am dead already, but I don't think so. I still want too much to be dead, to be content to be passive for eternity. Most of all I want Scotty to come home and say it's okay, everything's okay, and really mean it.

"We're going to light every corner, there won't be any dark places of ignorance," he said once, home on vacation from MIT. "It's ignorance that is the threat to the world, and unless we banish it in our lifetimes, the world will sink. It can't last with ignorant people in charge of such tremendous power. They don't understand power and the damage it can do."

Light every corner, I repeat here in the darkness; let no wall of shadows remain, and what will the illumination reveal? Only what man himself built. That which is hunted is destroyed by the search. What Scotty wants is the final truth, the final reason, and he can't have them. He forgets the other truths that lie useless and discarded, that were the causes of celebrations in other days, and knows this time we are truly on the path to enlightenment.

During his adolescence Scotty was uneasy with me, always darting quick glances to the others at dinner, especially the men, as if trying to guess which ones I might have slept with. Ask, I wanted to shout at him. It isn't like you think. Just ask. He couldn't ask, and I found I couldn't bring it up unless he did ask, no matter how indirectly. Then it was Kenneth he hated the most.

I wonder if it has occurred to Scotty that he is now the age Kenneth was when he first came to our house and stayed.

It was long after midnight. There was a fog so thick it seemed to be pressing the French doors inward; it muffled the world. The last light had gone off upstairs a few minutes earlier and the fog had become more solid, as if the light streaming out from the second floor had been a warning that finally had proven empty. The long table was covered with Rudy Levitsky's etchings, the desk with untidy piles of yellow and white paper. A sheet of yellow paper was in the typewriter, half filled, with many words Xed out. I was at the card table with scissors, paste, a manuscript, and some advertising material. I can still visualize the table, the entire room down to the crumbling log in the fireplace, burning with a pale orange glow. I don't know what I was working on, but it was like that month after month. The good days and weeks and months leave so little impression, they blend one into another, and there is a feeling of contentment, of peace, that revives with the memory of them. It had been like that since I had become the editor of the magazine. Peace, contentment, joy in work I was proud of. Joy in the people I worked with.

He must have tapped on the window several times before I became aware of it, for when I did, it was with a feeling of annoyance, as if an irritant had persisted a long time. No one could claim a lost key, I thought grumpily, God knew the place was never locked. I stamped to the windows. His face was pressed to the glass, as if the fog forced him tight against it. I didn't recognize him until I yanked open the door and he stumbled into the room.

"Kenneth! For heaven's sake! What are you doing here at this hour?"

"Why are you sitting in a lighted room with the drapes open and the doors unlocked? I could have walked right in and done terrible things to you. I could have cut your throat."

He was carrying a briefcase. There were water beads on his eyebrows, glistening in his bushy hair, which was wilder than ever from the moisture of the fog. His face was gray, there were deep black circles under his eyes. He put the briefcase down and flexed his fingers as he spoke. He swayed slightly and I caught his arm.

"Sit down. What's wrong? How did you get up here?"

"Walked, bus. I brought you something."

He started to reach for the case, but I pushed him toward the fire instead. "It'll keep. You're freezing and soaking wet. Strip. I'll go upstairs and get you a robe to put on." I started toward the door. "No bus comes up here. What do you mean, bus?"

"From Dallas. Walked up from the station. I'm strapped."

I hurried upstairs and got him one of Maury's robes. While he was getting out of his wet things, I made scrambled eggs and brewed coffee and we ate together before the fire. He had added logs to it, and now it roared and the room was too hot.

"How long were you on the bus?"

"I don't know. Two, three days."

"Is that how you're going to tell me about it? In driblets when I ask questions? It will take all night that way."

"I'm busted," he said. "Finished. I'm blacklisted, haven't worked in a couple of years, and decided to hell with it."

"Blacklisted! You! For God's sake, why?"

He shrugged. "Nothing. You've known me a long time, you know nothing, but how can anyone prove nothing? It can't be done. I bought as much film as I could afford, the bus ticket back home to Seattle, and I'll work up there taking kids' pictures in a dime store, or something."

"Where's Shelley?"

"She couldn't stand the gaff. Can't blame her. It's been rough, sort of."

"She's left you? Shelly? What do they say you did?"

"Meetings back in 1939, through the war years, you know the kind of stuff they spring. Where were you on January 19, 1939? How the hell do I know? I was in high school in 1939." He was glassy-eyed with fatigue.

"Let's get you to bed. We'll talk tomorrow."

"First, my present." He nearly fell when he leaned over to pick up the briefcase. He took out a folder and handed it to me. "Where's a bed?"

I took him to the third floor and saw him to bed and then went back down and looked inside the folder. It was a series of photographs he had taken of Scotty and me over the past seven years since we had first met him. I had known in a vague way that he was taking our pictures, he was always taking pictures of everyone. There were twelve eight-by-ten photographs. My favorite is one that was taken from behind us. We are walking on the beach, hand in hand, I am looking down at Scotty, his face is tilted up toward me. Later, I asked Kenneth to enlarge it; it hangs on my bedroom wall.

After he had rested I told Kenneth I wanted a picture story about bridges, starting with the Golden Gate Bridge.

He grinned and shook his head. "Sorry. I'm on my way to Seattle."

"Bullshit! You're giving up! This is a legitimate offer for a job I want done. I've been wanting it for a year and haven't found anyone who sees bridges the way I do. You can do it. I can't pay you what you're used to getting, but I do pay, half in advance, the balance on acceptance."

He smiled and kissed my cheek. "I love you dearly, Emily. I won't do it to you."

"You let me take care of me. You just do the job."

"Let's put it off until you talk to the colonel. Then we'll see."

"I have editorial autonomy. That was agreed when I took the position. He has nothing to do with what goes in the magazine."

"Talk to him."

"I'm going to New York next week. I'll see him. Will you stay here until I get back?"

The colonel had retired, had let his daughter persuade him to give up his bachelor apartment, move to her spacious home in the Village, and take life easy in his declining years.

He had sat in the park for four days, then had started looking for something to do and had acquired a paperback book company that he was running. He was busier than ever.

"Too damn much work," he grumbled over lunch. "Too old for so damn much work."

"Then quit."

"Can't quit. You know what I heard in the park? I heard the trees whispering about me, they said I'd last one month without work. Right, too."

"Colonel, I have a problem. I need help. Will you stop talking and listen to me for a change?"

"You know, Emily, you're your father made over. He used to do me exactly like that. No one wants to hear an old man talk."

"You're not an old man, and you talk too damn much."

He chuckled and motioned the waiter over. "We'll need another bottle of that Beaujolais. She's getting wound up."

I lighted a cigarette and he lighted a cigar and I lost that round too. The waiter returned and opened another bottle; before he could pour it, the colonel waved him away. "Not too hasty, son," he said, "give it time to catch its breath. Emily, ever tell you about the ladies on Park Avenue?"

I shook my head.

"Back when your father was a greenhorn in New York, 1900, before he married your mother. I told him he should get a wife, settle down, and he made grumbling noises about how the ladies like tall men, and he was too ugly anyway to get anyone worth carrying home." The colonel was in good form, his eyes distant, a smile playing over his face mischievously.

"Well, he was right, in a way," the colonel said. "The ladies didn't shine to him much, but not because he was short, because he was so confoundedly shy. He would lose his tongue as soon as a skirt got near him and not find it again until sometime the next morning. And he'd blush. He was too old to blush like a schoolboy, but he fired up with no provocation at all." The colonel chuckled and poured the wine. "It was his confidence that needed a hand, I decided, and I set about to find a way to help him over the hump. I decided to hire three young ladies, of a certain repute, if you understand. . . ." I nodded and he chuckled again. "I paid them to station themselves along Park Avenue, about a block apart one fine Friday evening when we were going to be strolling that way. When we came into view the first lady was to give William the eye, really give it to him, even drop her hankie, if the occasion rose. The next one was to move toward us, manage to bump into him and fuss over him a little. The last one was to strike up a conversation, walk with us a little ways and let him know without qualification that she thought he was the right sort of fellow."

I was laughing by then. "That was a terrible thing to do to him! That was really rotten!"

He nodded cheerfully. "Well, Friday came along, the way it does, and we were taking our stroll just as we had planned, and Ginger was where she was supposed to be, and everything went according to the schedule. William might have puffed his chest out a bit more, strutted a bit more, nothing noticeable, not yet. But he was more amiable after that. Then the second lady did her part, and now William was giving me the eye to make sure I was noticing what was happening, and I was clapping him on the back and telling him what a lady killer he had turned into. Just like the script called for. Then Marie practically kidnapped him, nearly dragged him into a storefront to hold an intimate little conversation with him, and after that he was glowing and his feet weren't touching the ground at all." He poured more wine and swirled it about. "I loved William like a brother. Still think of him as kin. Funny how that happens with some people, isn't it?" I nodded.

"Well, back to the story. We walked along for another block and hot damn if another little lady—one not quite so obviously of a certain repute as the other three had been—didn't turn up and start talking to William, all smiles and butter-wouldn't-melt-in-her-mouth cool. William got rid of her and there was another lady, and still another one, and I thought I'd lost track of how many I'd hired, but even when I thought that, I knew it wasn't so, because I didn't know more than three ladies of that sort that I could hire. All in all that evening William was flirted with by at least seven and maybe eight young ladies, and he took it as if he were the Prince of Wales and this a daily occurrence. And I was getting a little disgruntled because no matter what I did, not one of them even glanced at me." He laughed hard and wiped his eyes with the back of his hand. "He had heard from one of my ladies what I was doing and did me one better and hired some others that he knew to carry the charade even further."

"What do you mean seven or eight?"

"Well, we counted later and we both thought there was a legitimate lady in the crowd, but she got lost in the shuffle."

After a moment he reached across the table and patted my hand. "Now a man who'd do all that for a friend isn't likely to turn down that friend's daughter, is he? What is the problem, Emily?"

"I want to use photographs by Kenneth Cruze, and he is on the blacklist."

"Ah." For several minutes we were both silent and finally he asked, "Why did you come to me about it? Why didn't you just go on and use the pictures?"

"He won't do it without your knowledge. He said it could be damaging for you. There's nothing to it! I've known him for seven years and I believe him."

"What are they saying about him?"

"The usual. Meetings back in 1939—when he was a

highschool boy! More meetings during the war years—
when he was in the army!"

"Doesn't signify," he said. "Okay, use the pictures. You
could lose the magazine, you know that. If we lose too
much advertising, the magazine folds."

"You wouldn't carry it a while, even if I take a cut in
salary?"

"He means that much to you?"

I shook my head. "Yes and no. He's totally apolitical.
He just doesn't notice. He's an artist, and he is going to
win the Pulitzer one of these years if he can keep away
from commercial crap awhile. He is an explorer in his
field, leading the others by a mile. He deserves the opportunity to keep going. That's what he means to me. Did
you know Gloria Woodson—she married Sam Laski?"

He shook his head.

"She saved my life back in the thirties. Everything had
caved in, Father died, my mother was gone, everything
was gone, and I was broke. Really down to nothing, no
job, no hope. Nothing. I would have died, I think.

I drank wine, he poured more. "I had a tiny apartment,
a dismal tenement apartment that Mother had been shar-
ing with me. She left to move in with Randolf and I lay
down on the couch and slept. A day, two days, three, I
don't know how many days I slept. I'd get up, drink tea
until it was gone, then water, go to the bathroom down
the hall, go back to sleep. How could anyone sleep like
that?"

"You weren't sleeping," the colonel said. "You just
stopped awhile."

"I suppose. I don't think I even felt hungry, I wasn't
thinking about anything at all, not wanting anything. It
was strange, just strange. Anyway, Gloria came looking
for me, and that was strange too. She never had done that
before. She didn't even know my mother had left." I
stopped, remembering. Gloria had been blond and plump
and soft-looking, very fair, with a complexion like a der-
matologist's ideal. We had worked together for an advertising agency that pushed mink coats and Cadillacs and
other luxury items until 1929, when suddenly the money
vanished. She had found work with a publisher and I
hadn't. We shared an apartment until my mother was
forced to move in with me.

"You were calling for help," the colonel said softly, breaking into my reverie. "And she heard."

"Do you really think that?"

"Yes."

"Then I can believe it too. Anyway, Gloria hauled me out of there, took me in, kept me going until I found a job. I went to some meetings with her, youth rallies for jobs, things like that. She was active in organizing unions, too, I think. Then she got a better job, and met Sam Laski, and I got a full-time job, and things were looking up generally, and we both dropped all that. It was desperation, the times, the climate. You know."

He nodded. "I know, honey. Go on."

"She went into television after the war, producer, editor, I don't know what all. They named her, drove her out of her work, out of her mind. I lived with her those years, I know it was a lie. She was not a Communist or even a sympathizer. She took an overdose. I didn't even know it was happening until it was almost over. That's what it means to me."

"They could put you on the list," the colonel said soberly.

"They will! They will put everyone on that damn list, everyone who doesn't bow down to them, doesn't scrape his forehead on the ground, kiss asses! I won't! I'd rather start the fight than wake up one morning and see my name in the papers like Gloria did."

"What the hell," he said then. "You've already put your head on the block with your editorials. Didn't want to bring them up before, but damnit, Emily, look up the word *discretion* in your little pocket dictionary someday, will you. Kenneth Cruze, you say. Seem to recall seeing some of his work in *Life*, or *Look*, or someplace like that. Does he have enough stuff to put together to make a book? Tell him to bundle it up and send me a sample if he thinks there's enough. An oversized paperback, coffee-table-type book. Not a lot of money in it, but sometimes there's prestige. That's what trashy bestsellers are for—to give you money to play around with for those things you know won't make you a dime. Pity they're in the majority. My God, where do all the new writers come from? You wouldn't believe how many people think they can write books, send you garbage they call novels, or histories, or whatever, and sit back waiting to get rich and famous.

Bah! Universal education inflates people's heads, makes them think getting the diploma gives them license to sell every precious word they can put on paper."

"He's probably a Commie," Scotty said sullenly when I told him and Dorrie we might be in for trouble.

"Don't be ridiculous," I snapped at him, tired of his surliness, his poorly veiled dislike of Kenneth. "He was sixteen when they say he got involved. Can you imagine yourself getting involved in politics? And even if you did get an idealistic itch, what would it mean? Would that make you a threat to the national security?"

"You don't know what he's done since then," Scotty said. "They don't just draw names out of hats, you know. They have evidence or they would be afraid they'd get sued or something."

"They don't! That's the whole point. They don't have diddly squat!"

"I don't know why you're bothering to tell us anything about it," he said, not looking at me. "You'll do what you want anyway."

"Because I want you to know they will attack me, that's their style. They'll call me Communist, sympathizer, traitor. They'll attack me on personal grounds. Things could become nasty and I want to prepare you, to let you know—"

"Things are already nasty! Why'd he come here? We don't need him! Why don't you just tell him to get out of here!"

"Scotty! What are you implying! What do you mean?"

"Shut up! Will you! Just shut up and leave me alone!"

He ran from the room and I heard the double door open and slam shut. "He thinks that Kenneth and I . . ."

"That too, I guess," Dorrie said. She looked unhappy and I knew this was almost as hard on her as it was on me. "But it's more than that, I think. I remember when I was his age, that's when I left home. It's a bloody awful age. You start seeing people in a new way. I couldn't stand my mum and dad."

"I'll change," I said. "I'll become a model of middle-class virtues for him to rebel against, and then when he becomes human I'll take off the mask and we'll be friends."

Dorrie snorted and stood up. "And I'll grow a beard.

Anyway, I'm glad Kenneth's away taking pictures. That'll give *him* time to cool off a little."

"But there's nothing between Kenneth and me"

"I know that. But he doesn't, and there's no way you could convince him. Maybe Kenneth will be busy for a good long time."

Having Kenneth gone didn't improve anything, however. Scotty sulked, and when the spring vacation came he refused to go back to the Oregon desert with me, a trip we had planned off and on for a year.

We had gone the year before, and he had panned for gold in the John Day River. His hair was bleached out almost gold that summer, the last year it was really light, and I watched it reflect back the golden sunlight as he squatted, tilting the pan around this way and that, scowling with concentration. I was startled by his yelp of triumph when he found a few grains of gold in the pan. We had gone on through Picture Gorge the next day, examined the ancient pictographs and talked about how the land must have been when the Indians were the only people on it. He had become silent and withdrawn then, until in camp he announced, "I'm going to be a geologist too."

We dug for fossils, fonud carnelian and sagenitic agate, searched for and didn't find sunstones and opals, and for two weeks we lived apart from the world, content, at peace.

He would not repeat the adventure.

"Why not, Scotty? You know you had a great time."

"That was last year. Things are different."

"What's different?"

"Everything."

I was in his room, standing at the open door. He had models hanging from the ceiling and on the desk—airplanes, cars, rockets. He was working on a radio kit then, and parts were scattered on a card table; his phonograph was blaring; books were on the bed and the floor alongside it.

"Mind if I sit down a minute?"

He glanced around and we both knew there was no place anyone could sit without rearranging everything first. He made no motion to do that. "If you want to. I've gotta go out, though."

"Go where? It's after ten."

"Eddie Foster's house. We're going fishing with his father and Gary next week."

Myron Foster was a lawyer and a state representative. He lived with his wife and two sons above us on the hill in a new, expensive ranch house that sprawled half a city block. They had a swimming pool, and Mrs. Foster gave parties for the boys, let them grill steaks outside, play pool or cards in the rec room. Gary was seventeen and seemed always in trouble at school, or with the police over his driving, or something else. At first Scotty had spoken of his escapades with contempt, then with a touch of admiration, and, most recently, I realized, not at all.

"It's too late to go out now, Scotty," I said.

"Just to Eddie's house."

"It'll keep until tomorrow."

"I'm not a baby!" he shouted. "Don't treat me like a baby!"

I closed the door. "What are you yelling about, for heaven's sake? You know you can't go out when it's almost ten-thirty. Be reasonable."

"You think I'm a baby. You always do. You think I don't know anything, understand anything. And you're wrong. I know what's going on around here all the time! I'm not a little kid anymore!"

"What do you think is going on?"

"I'm going over to Eddie's."

"You are not."

He took a step toward the door, where I stood with the knob hard against the small of my back, hurting me. I didn't move. Abruptly he pivoted and swept the books from his bed, making them sail across the room. "I'm going to bed."

"I want to talk about this."

"I'm tired."

"There's nothing going on around here to upset you. Nothing. I don't know what you think you know, but nothing is going on."

He threw himself face down on the bed and pulled the pillow over his ears. Not a baby? I wanted to spank him or hug him until he relented and told me what was bothering him. He didn't move. When I finally went to the bed and sat by him, he jerked away and lay on the extreme edge.

"Scotty, just talk about it, please. This is silly. How can I explain, or deny, or even admit anything if I don't know what it is?"

After a long silence, I asked, "Is it Kenneth? There's nothing but friendship between us, honey. He is a dear friend, no more than that."

He had moved the pillow a bit; he was listening.

"Honey, a lot of people move into and out of our lives. Kenneth is broke, out of a job, he needs friends now. What kind of a friend would I be if I turned my back on him?"

"He's a Communist," Scotty said, the pillow muffling his words. "Everyone knows that."

"No one knows that because it isn't true. Who told you it was?"

"Everyone."

"Who, Scotty? Not everyone. Just one person. Who?"

The pillow went down hard again and he wouldn't talk to me anymore. Foster, I thought with contempt. That bastard Foster, with his bigger-than-life American flag fluttering in his yard, and his bigger-than-life mouth spouting nonsense about loyalty oaths for teachers and students and visiting lecturers at the university. The Foster boys never came to our house, and Scotty was spending more and more of his time at theirs.

He was barely civil at home during the next few months; his face was drawn into a sullen scowl most of the time, and he spoke only to answer direct questions, and then in the curtest, most direct answers.

"I think he's sick," I said to Dorrie late one night. "He needs a doctor, a psychiatrist, or a counselor, or something."

"He needs a wallop on the behind," Dorrie said. "That kid's heading for real trouble if he doesn't shape up."

"It's adolescence, I know, but my God, does it have to be this hard?"

"It's pure and simple meanness. He's making you pay for not giving him a father, that's all it is."

I stared at her and numbly accepted what she said.

If it hadn't been for Dr. Frederick Tissot, I think Scotty would have ended up in a juvenile court. His grades were slipping disastrously; he had been in two accidents, not as a driver yet, but we all knew that would come soon enough. And he was staying out until all hours without telling me where he was going or whom he was with.

Dr. Tissot called me and asked if I could meet with him. He was a professor of geology at Berkeley, had studied under my father and had never forgotten him. My father had taken his class out to study Lassen Peak, he told me, and he had been changed from that day.

"I'm planning an expedition to Africa, Mrs. Carmichael. For the same purpose, to study an active volcano, and I am emulating your father's example and taking a group of students with me. Scotty was recommended most highly by his school, and although he will be the youngest boy in the group, in view of the fact that he is his grandfather's heir, so to speak, and in acknowledgment of my own debt to your father, I am willing to include him, if you consent."

There were conferences. His school agreed to grant him the leave, if he pulled himself together, straightened out, got his grades back up to his usual level, stopped being tardy, and playing hooky, etc., etc. Overnight he did all those things.

Dorrie and I scraped and schemed to get the money together, and I had to borrow against the house, but we did it, and when Scotty was sixteen he went to Tanganyika with Dr. Tissot and nineteen other students.

I wept and Dorrie wept with me the night he left; it was the first time he had been away from us. And actually not much had changed. He still despised Kenneth and refused to speak to him any more than a grunt of hello or a mumbled something when Kenneth passed the salt, or made any other human gesture toward him. He had watched the HUAC demonstrations and called the students radicals and terrorists, and he spoke bitterly of my involvement, my editorials and the articles I ran.

"It doesn't seem fair, Emily, it sure doesn't seem fair," Dorrie said. "For fifteen, sixteen years you give them everything, more than you can, even, and they just leave you cold. And you don't have anything at all."

"He'll be back, Dorrie. It's just six weeks." But we both knew he would never really be back, not as he had once been.

He went away to MIT the next year and hasn't involved himself in politics or peace demonstrations, or anything else except his work, since then. And we haven't become friends yet.

We don't fight, and I think it would be better if we did. We are very polite to each other, never forget holidays, birthdays, things of that sort. He sends me lovely presents, and visits once a year, and now and then even calls to tell me he's up from the bottom of the sea, or that he'll be in the Azores for a few months, or something. And we are not friends.

For years I thought he didn't even read the magazine, but Cissy, his first wife, said he did, from cover to cover, and then threw it out. She came to me when they separated.

"I love him, Emily," she said. "But he won't let me love him. He keeps me so far away. I begged him to get help and he was furious with me. But I can't stand it! I'm starting to feel like I'm made out of ice too, all frozen smiles and don't touch and watch for a thaw when suddenly he's a different person altogether. I just can't stand it."

He married again, this time to a very proper young woman who wanted their marriage to remain on an intellectual plane. She didn't like me, and she didn't come to me when they separated, but she wrote me a letter. It was my fault. He was a madman, a lustful, sexually perverted madman, and I should be ashamed for setting the example for him that I did. I laughed and wept alternately over her letter for days until Dorrie took it away and burned it.

I can think that each of us has to find a way through this maze and there never is any outside help, not really. But the guilt rises and washes over the rational thoughts and I want only to go back and do something over again, differently next time, but I don't know which thing.

When we went to the beach he loved that the most, and when we went to the mountains he loved them the most. Shrieking with glee in the surf, or wading icy streams intent on finding a bit of gold in the rocky bottom, staring in awe at the whales offshore, touching delicately a chipmunk he had enticed to our campfire with chocolate-covered peanuts, the images flood in, clear, sharp, immediate. His head at the level of my breasts, up to my shoulders, his eyes on a level with mine—it was all too fast, too terribly fast.

"What's a bastad?" He was belligerent, defiant, ready to fight, standing in the doorway to my study. He was ten.

I put down the copy I had been editing. "A what?" But I knew. "You mean bastard." I motioned him in. "A long

time ago when there were knights and kings and noble-
men, it was the custom for royalty to marry only into
other royal families. Suppose a nobleman, a prince say,
fell in love with a girl who was not of a king's family,
they wouldn't have been allowed to marry. Often they
lived together anyway because they loved each other
deeply, and no one thought that was wrong. If they had
children, they were called bastards. Being a bastard was a
high honor because it meant a nobleman had loved your
mother, and the child had royal blood."

"Why does Grandma call me a poor bastard?"

"Oh, Scotty. Come sit down." I went to the fireplace
and sat on the couch. He continued to stand in the center
of the room. "Your grandmother is sick, honey. Sometimes she says things she shouldn't and she can't help it."
He didn't move. That wasn't answering his question and
he knew it. "Your father and I loved each other very
much. He was a soldier, I told you that, a pilot. We were
going to get married on his next leave, but he was shot
down before we could."

"Was he a nobleman?"

"Not like in the old days. But noble means good and
very honorable and kind, and he was noble. He was a very
good, very brave man, a hero during the war. You can be
very proud of your father, darling."

He sat down at the far end of the couch and for a long
time didn't say anything. Then: "If he wasn't killed we
would be English, wouldn't we. I'd talk like Dorrie."

He asked more questions and I told him everything I
had been able to find out about Leslie Scott, RAF captain
killed in action in October 1939, whom I had never met.

That was the one lie I ever told him, one monstrous lie,
and lived the rest of my life with him in absolute honesty.
Sometimes I think the honesty was more damaging, sometimes I know it was the lie that separated us. Sometimes it
has chilled me to think he could have seen into the future,
could have seen that Kenneth and I were to become lovers
even though at the time he made the implicit accusation,
we were still no more than friends. Like my mother, I
thought, seeing that Jason and I were more than friends,
and banished the thoughts, forced them out of existence
for a time. Now, bound to my earthquake-damaged house,
waiting for Help, who is abnormally slow this long night, I

can't banish any thoughts at all. I have become an eye, wafted this way and that, riding the currents of time, seeing more than I want to see, remembering more than I want to remember.

11

"Emily, come to Mexico with me." Kenneth stood before the French windows, looking out at the terrace, which was covered with an inch of water. The rain was steady, had been steady for days.

I didn't move for what seemed a long time, my pencil poised over the manuscript I was working on, a story by Marguerite Schachtel, who writes under the by-line of Vincent Gary and does devastatingly funny stories about public figures. The one I was editing was about Billy Cracker, who chats with God and gets his approval for various questionable practices of the government and passes on this approval in his sermons.

"It isn't gratitude," Kenneth said, still at the window. "You get first crack at whatever I do, that's gratitude and loyalty and devotion. What I'm suggesting now is simple love."

I turned to stare at him. His head was too large for his body, silhouetted as he was against the light, with his hair uncut, standing out in every direction. He looked like a boy. "You saved my ass four years ago," he said, his face hidden in shadows, his voice grave. "I'll be indebted to you forever and you know that. It's made it damn hard to ask you to go to bed with me, though."

Then I laughed and for a moment he thought I was laughing at him, then he didn't think that and we went to Mexico. He took pictures of ruins and I watched him and studied the ruins and thought curious thoughts.

Sooner or later it comes to this, ruins that other people trample over and study for clues about what happened, and how to avoid letting it happen again. Of course, it can't happen to our civilization; we are lighting the dark forests, illuminating every shadowed corner. It can't happen to us. I was silent and thoughtful in our room that evening.

"It gets me too," Kenneth said. "They were the tops, the highest. Then nothing. It's scary."

"How many times has it happened? We know so little about the past. Some ruined Thai temples, the Aztecs, a few stone formations here and there. How many times? Why?"

He sat at the window, looking at the sunset on the mountains. "You'll drive yourself nuts trying to puzzle it out."

"It's because they built on air. Nothing but air. Hot air of false premises, and one day the wind changed and the castles toppled."

"Emily, Relax. Sit by me and look at the sunset. It's incredible."

I sat by him and he took my hand. "It's true anyway," I said. He nodded and turned again to the vista of jungle and mountains and sunset. "It's true," I said, to myself. And we were doing it again.

"Once they believed that Earth must have passed through regions in space where there was tremendous heat, and that accounted for the interior heat of the planet that still erupts in volcanoes," my father said. "That seemed plausible enough at the time, they could accept that and live with it. Even explain many of the puzzles with it." He laughed. "They refused to look at the little details, you see. They could accept the grand theories and never had to look at the details, because the unifying theories were so sweeping, they explained everything. What a comfort that must have been for them."

"And now you know better," I say in the darkness, and his voice is there.

"Yes, we do. You have to look at the details and piece them together and only then make a general statement. We know that now."

Scotty's voice is nearby too. "They tried," he says with a touch of scorn and impatience. "They just didn't have the tools, the computers, the technology. . . ." He is talking about my father.

"Emily, what's wrong? You've been staring out there for half an hour without saying a word." Kenneth again, back in Mexico.

"I'm scared, really scared."

"Of what? For Christ's sake, what's there to be scared of?"

"I don't know."

Is that what Jason fought and gave into—something he couldn't even name?

"We have to learn everything and then we can make predictions, have some kind of control, and the world will be a safer place." Scotty again. Predict and control. But he got caught in the rain that day, and his wife left him a month later, and Johnson was following the Goldwater scenario. "We don't mean things like that," he says here in the darkness, very impatient with me. "You know what I mean."

He means things like eclipses, and high and low tides, and spring frosts and the effectiveness of insecticides and fungicides and an automobile's miles per gallon and the date of the windows that open to a Mars flight and how much radiation a person can tolerate before it kills him and the trajectory of a bomb and how to test a foetus for abnormalities. . . . And knowing all that, and much much more, would not have kept Cissy in his bed, would not allow him to enter my house without that rapid search to see who else is there, would not prevent the terror of possible nuclear war from influencing his actions, invading his dreams.

"Emily, are you all right?" Kenneth brought me a drink and sat before me, studying my face. "What is it?"

"I don't know. You. Scotty. Me. Everything seems somehow tied together with those ruins, and it's frightening."

"I didn't drive Scotty away, you know."

I knew that. Scotty left because of me, because he couldn't bear to have his mother so out of step with the world that he was shamed by her over and over. He left because his adolescent indignation had never turned outward to greater injustices, but had remained focused on his intimate relationships with his mother, and with a father he never had and whose existence he always doubted. Scotty left because I never learned to sew a hem.

"Emily, you're shaking. Are you sick?"

Kenneth touched my cheek and his hand felt cold. "You're feverish. You are ill."

"No. It's nothing. It's the ruins, the ghosts among the ruins, all searching for something, forever searching. . . ."

That night the ghosts walked in procession up the steep stairs to the top of the pyramid, an endless stream of ghosts, silent, harming no one, doing nothing except climbing the stairs to the top, where they vanished as more and more of them crowded together at the bottom, forever moving upward.

I woke up with Kenneth's hands on my shoulders.

"You were dreaming," he said. "Can you talk about it now?"

"I don't know what it is."

"In the end it doesn't matter," he said, lighting a cigarette for himself, another for me. "People think whatever is accepted and behave according to customs, and believe this superficial overlay is all of life. Sooner or later they all face whatever it was you saw. Some will be destroyed by it, others will forget it instantly, their conditioning stronger than it is, and some, like you, will learn to live with it. But it doesn't matter. You can't change anything. You just do the best you can, live day to day. What more can there be?"

I left Kenneth in Mexico and flew home. He agreed that I should leave, and he didn't try to go with me. "It's your fight right now," he said. "No one can help you."

Maury said, "You've tasted mortality. It scared you."

"Not that. Not that."

"Menopause then."

So easy to dismiss the terror with catch words— *mortality, menopause*. I saw doctors and took hormones, tranquilizers, and sleeping pills, and started at sounds in the night, the ghosts that prowled the house. I would have quit the magazine if I hadn't mortgaged the house again for Scotty's education. And somehow I got through the year and the next. The terror was my constant companion, one that could not be talked about or mentioned because it was nameless. Kenneth, I think, understood because he doesn't rely on words, on linear constructions to comprehend the world. And we couldn't talk about it.

Something is spinning about me, closer, then farther away, casting a bluish-green light over everything. It spins faster and faster, and then stops and I can see that it is the world I gave Jason, the blue-green malachite world so finely carved into continents, mountains, shorelines. It is very beautiful.

It comes closer to me and grows larger, until I am part of it and now I am spinning too, and it casts me out to a point where I can observe it. How the surface shifts; it is not the still dead world I had thought. Its surface is alive, and I can look through the surface and see the life that goes through it to the center—boiling, furious motion, at first meaningless, but gradually taking on a form that is almost understandable.

I watch the bubbling together of rocks, minerals, the heavy material from deep within the globe. A golden river separates out and settles, another band of silver, of green, flecks of mica intrude into gray semisolid rock and the whole solidifies, covered with black volcanic rocks. Rain and wind work at breaking up the surface, soil is deposited, is blown away, deposited again, and this time is covered with lichens that hold it firmly, that reach out to hold other grains of soil. Mosses and ferns follow and find sustenance, then grasses and bushes, vines, trees. They grow up, die, fall, mix with the volcanic base. A great flood churns it all and, falling once more, leaves yet more detritus behind, and a new forest is born, only to be cleared, burned, plowed under so that grapes and lettuces and strawberries may grow. And they in turn yield to the ceaseless change. A new volcano buries everything and the cycles continue.

Suddenly I am with Kenneth watching a sunset that has turned a river into gold. Kenneth dips his hands into the water and lifts them. They are gilded, they gleam in the light of the red sun. He stares at them in wonder, but I am afraid. I don't want him to touch me with his golden hands. I run away in panic and it is in my own house that I am running, racing up and down hallways that have become infinitely long and mysterious. I make no sound, even the ghosts are stilled, and I know he is there behind me, trying to touch me with his terrifying hands.

"I can't photograph you," he complains. "What I capture is a stranger, someone I don't even know. You're never still enough to catch. You're the sum of too many shifting lines, lights, expressions that are too swift to get on film. What I do get is frozen and artificial, homely even, and you're not homely. You are very lovely and I think the loveliness is something that is invisible, it is something that affects those you are with and has nothing to do with your features at all. I can't explain it. I'm sorry these pictures are so awful. I'll try again. I'll catch you yet, when you're not expecting it, when you forget the camera."

The air is soft and cool, rich with sea smells. Although it is dark, the middle of the night, I am struck by the beauty of the water. The colors change from blue to green to shades in between that I can't name, with white streaks and gray shadows, and there is a constant motion that plays with the colors, trying different combinations, different depths. I can't tell where the water stops and the air begins and I narrow my eyes trying to discern the one spot, the one point of demarcation that separates sea from air. There is no such place. I follow the water to the shore and again there is no place where sea stops and sand begins. They flow together, partake of each other, and farther inland, the grasses and trees are of the sand, of the rocks and cliffs, and there is nothing that is alone and separate; everything flows into everything else. Just as the blue and green and white foam are of the sea, so are the sea and sand and trees and cliffs part of . . . part of . . . I try to see my own arm and it is part of the sky, of trees, of sand and sea and beach and pebbles and driftwood and fishes. . . .

It is gone. Everything is gone and I am here again in the darkness suspended in time. What brought me back? I can hear a sound that wasn't here before. Rain. It is starting to rain. The rain is hard, driving, I can hear it beating against the house.

Poor Mr. Rossiter. All his work wrenched apart, now getting soaked, as if whatever damage the earthquake left undone must now be finished. I hope he is well insured, but I doubt it. The cost of insurance in earthquake country is high; possibly he, even as I, decided it is

too high; we'll take our chances, Mr. Rossiter and I. We
understand this country, Mr. Rossiter and I; we submit to
it, accept its terms. And now the rains will work to heal
the scars, in a false repentance that is a mockery.

If the quake was very small, the epicenter out at sea,
then probably no one will come this way in days. If it was
very large, racing along the fault lines all the way to Los
Angeles, then no one will come in days because the cities
will demand all available aid. Like Goldilocks, I hope for
just the right size, a middling earthquake, because I know
I cannot endure this even a few more hours, much less
days. I suppose the end will come during a hallucination.
I'll float away and never come back and all in all that is
not a bad way to go. Suddenly it seems very unimportant
to make my peace with Scotty first.

It's absurd that I should have tried to make Scotty
happy, force him to adopt an attitude that would permit
him to experience happiness. That is funny. No more,
Scotty, wherever you are, no more. You're on your own,
darling. It's up to you.

I am very tired, more tired than I've ever been, I think.
I'll sleep, and this time I'll dream of a happy time, a time
when Jason and I danced all night and made love at
dawn.

Actually I dreamed of a field of golden corn, no leaves
or plants, only gleaming crafted ears of corn, and I
wanted one of them desperately. I woke with the hot
pleasure/pain of desire that only gradually subsided. All
my life people have been telling me it's wrong, sinful, evil,
immoral, unethical, and disgusting for a woman to admit
she feels sexual desire for a man. Now that it is admitted
that women are also sexual creatures, it is still wrong
for me, because I am too old.

"Why don't you for God's sake marry him?" Scotty
talking about Tony. Marry him and settle down and stop
making a fool of yourself, is what he was thinking, what
he would have said if he had had the courage.

If I marry Tony, Scotty will be happy, and he will stop
hating Tony so much. He will be able to pretend to himself and the world that I married for security in my old
age. That is acceptable.

My sister, Wanda, has been a widow for ten years and
she told me there had been no sex for at least ten years
before Thomas died. He had a bad heart. Because they

were afraid having sex would kill him, they didn't, and he died anyway. Wanda is busy with her children's lives, with her grandchildren, with her garden club and various charities. She knits and crochets beautifully. She does not visit me very often. She says my household makes her nervous. They hang around, she says, because it's free. Moochers, all of them. Even Kenneth? I asked her. "Even Kenneth. He's pathetic, hanging around a woman your age. What's wrong with him?" Kenneth and I had had our brief affair and were by then only friends. I didn't tell her that. She would not have believed it.

Randolf comes more often, and sits with a sad little smile on his face and mumbles at anyone who will stop to listen to him. He talks about our childhood in the house, and that makes me sad because it suggests that he has had nothing since then to sustain him. No now, no tomorrow, no recent past, only his childhood.

Wanda lectured me for several years about Scotty, then gave that up, and started on me directly. She means well, she always reminds me, she doesn't want to make me mad, but . . .

"It ruined your life, going off with Father every summer like you did," Wanda once said angrily. "You won't listen to anyone, you won't follow the rules, you won't behave like other women. It isn't fair!" she cried, and this was the real reason for her resentment. "You've been able to live your life like a man, with no responsibilities at all. If we all lived like you do, there wouldn't be any civilization!"

"What do you mean responsibility? I've made my own way all my life. I pay my bills, I educated Scotty."

"I don't mean that. You've always made good money. I know that. But you've never had to be responsible for someone else first. You come and go when you get ready, never answer to anyone. You've never acted like a woman in your life. You're not interested in women's things. I can't imagine you ever think of yourself as a woman at all."

"Wanda, I've done something to hurt you, haven't I? What? What did I do?" I tried to think what I had done or said and nothing came. Wanda looked very much like our mother then, stiff, put-upon, unyielding. Maybe I had not reacted enthusiastically enough to something she had said about one of the grandchildren.

"It's your attitude," she said. "Just like Tom's used to be

when I showed him something I had made. Contemptuous. He never could be bothered to pay attention either. As if to say, you poor ninny, don't waste my time with your silly things."

Her shawl. She had mentioned that she had crocheted it, and I had said it was lovely. Not enough, obviously. But why not? What else was required? I should have fingered it, examined the stitches, as Dorrie had done. I said, "I don't know the first thing about crocheting, you know that. All I can say is it's lovely. I don't know enough to say more. It's like looking at a bridge, how do I know if the suspension cables have too much tension? But a bridge architect knows. He'd talk about the length of the cables, or the number of posts, or the use of materials. Are the rest of us being contemptuous when we just say the bridge is a nice one, or is beautiful?"

"I'm not talking about bridges!" She stood up and began to gather together her things—purse, gloves, shawl. "You're impossible to talk to. It's like a different language. I feel sorry for you, Emily. The day will come when you'll regret your life. You'll wish you had grandchildren, something to occupy yourself with, find comfort in."

After she had left I thought about it. Responsibility. Not personal, not financial. Responsibility to her, to other women like her, to the perpetuation of the myth that women are subservient to men, have to consider them before making a move, that women have an innate knowledge about needlework and its importance in the scheme. Responsibility to the perpetuation of the myth that a woman can be fulfilled only through her children and their children, and her own busy hands. I thought, I must find time to be kinder to Wanda because she is so lonely and empty. And I thought of the fall of civilization because a person, especially a woman, gets out of line early and never finds her place in it again, and even comes to doubt the importance or necessity of the line. She was right, of course. If enough people come to doubt the importance of the line, that would be a threat to civilization.

I wish Jackie Wonder could hear that. "I'm a threat to civilization, Jackie Wonder! I don't live like other women. I refuse the role, always have. I love men, I love the earth and the sky and the ocean and the rocks and birds and animals! I even love women, you bloody asshole! I'm a threat to civilization!"

12

We drove into the mountains slowly on a warm June day with soft air and little wind. Past the national forest land where redwoods and Douglas firs grew luxuriantly, hinting of the paradise that had been. We turned off the interstate and onto a secondary road that twisted murderously, where logging trucks roared past us doing fifty miles an hour on a road posted for ten or fifteen. Maury drove cautiously, and in the back seat Scotty smoked and said nothing. He had not wanted to come. He was home for a short vacation only, recently separated from Cissy, and very unhappy. Maury had insisted that he come along.

"There's another turn off up ahead," Maury said. "It isn't on the road maps, a private road maintained only enough for the residents, not for tourists and loggers."

I glanced at Scotty, who gazed out the window. He was frowning. What a beautiful young man he had become. Tall and gracefully built, with nice light brown hair that waved just enough, and green-blue eyes, very straight eyebrows that bleached out almost white every summer. His description could have fit so many young men his age, I also thought, and wondered what it was that made each of them so different, although on paper, statistically, they were like peas.

We turned off again and this road was no more than a cleared space among the trees and rocks. We were in southern Oregon then, this forest was of Sitka spruce trees and rhododendrons. Up we twisted, then down again, back and forth until I lost what little sense of location I had had before. It was very wild, untouched-looking country. No houses with neat stacks of firewood and station wagons parked in the driveways. No gas stations and tourist-trap shops. No drive-in movies. Only trees and rocks. It seemed a long time before we turned finally onto a track even narrower and less maintained.

And there was the house. It was built of logs in part, fieldstone in part, added to at various times with no regard for what had gone before. There were two massive chimneys of gray rock, a wide porch on two sides, and shutters on all the windows. A stream ran along the side of the house, and there was a level yard where ground-covering ferns grew, an oasis in the wilderness.

"Come on in and look it over," Maury said. He was quiet and grim that day. It was 1965. I approached the house, feeling Maury's grimness invade me until by the time we got to the door I was glancing over my shoulder with apprehension, almost expecting to see enemies in the woods.

The door was steel, the shutters opened to reveal barred windows. The house was effectively sealed. Inside, it was cozy, with heavy furniture, plaid drapes of blue and gold, round woven rugs on the plank floors. There were six rooms and a full basement, and, Maury said, a second basement that extended out under the ground.

"We got through the missile crisis," Maury said, pouring bourbon for all of us. "I didn't think we would at the time. A lot of people didn't believe we would. If it gets that close again, we may not be so lucky. I want you both to have keys to this cabin and if you ever need to run, this will be here."

Scotty drank deeply and put his glass down hard, too hard. The noise made me jump. "Your idea of a bomb shelter?" he asked sarcastically. "Maury, come off it."

For years it had been Uncle Maury, but five or six years earlier he had dropped the Uncle. He was fond of Maury when he wasn't actively hating him, and he respected him through whatever other feelings came and went.

Maury nodded soberly. "Bomb shelter, a place to run to, whatever you want to call it. You know the way up here now, and you'll have a key. I don't care what you call it. If you ever need it, it's here. I'll keep it well stocked."

Scotty grinned and went to the door. "I'm going to have a look around. You were right about one thing. No one would ever find it without being brought up the first time."

"Scotty, wait a minute," I said. I had been watching Maury and I thought this was more than a reaction to the bomb scare. "What else do you think could send us running up here, Maury?"

"You remember Jason Mohr?" He was watching his hands as he poured another drink for himself.

For a moment I felt frozen. Not now! I wanted to scream at him. No confrontation now, not after all these years.

Maury didn't wait for a reply. "Jason Mohr was a great historian, philosopher, economist, I don't know which, or maybe a combination of the three," he said, looking at Scotty who was holding the doorknob, deliberately, almost contemptuously polite. "He wrote a book a long time ago, your mother helped him rewrite it. Remember Emily?" Again he didn't look at me. "In that book," Maury said, going now to sit down in one of the heavy chairs, "Jason predicted a good many things. Including the need for nearly constant war, for a war economy to feed a system that was even then showing signs of cancerous growth. And he predicted a bust that would follow the conclusion of active wars. If he'd had one foot in the future he couldn't have been more accurate in his predictions, right down the line, government, business, unionism, multinational corporations. He was a genius. A real genius."

He sighed and drank and I thought he was going to leave it at that. Then he looked at Scotty again and said, "I didn't believe all his forecasts, no man could have believed them all without wanting to commit suicide, which is what he did. He was like a man high in a building that he knows is going to erupt into flames at any time. He's tried to warn everyone and they wouldn't listen; they're talking about new fire extinguishers all the while that he's talking about a holocaust. He couldn't go on partying and drinking and making small talk with them, he couldn't ward off what he knew was coming, and in the end it killed him. I, and a lot of others like me, kept building bigger and better fire extinguishers, installing fire-resistant drapes, taking out more insurance. We couldn't believe that when it came, the fire would be bigger than our futile little plans could cope with."

I thought about the small gray church with the candles in the slit windows, remembered standing before it when it was a heap of rubble, and weeping.

Maury looked up and smiled gently at me. "I remember that Hanrahan didn't want to pay you for your work on the book. He wanted it burned. I made him give it to me. I intended to read it, but there was no time, and then Jason killed himself and I found I didn't want to read the manuscript after all. I put it away until a few years ago when I came across it again and this time read it. You did a magnificent job with him, Emily. A truly magnificent job."

"Maury, what's the point?" Scotty asked, his hand on the doorknob. "We got through the missile crisis, and other crises, and no doubt will again. So what's the point?"

"No point," Maury said after a hesitation. "You'll have the key if you want to use it. That's all."

Scotty shrugged and opened the door. "I'll be back in half an hour or so. I saw an outcropping I want to have a look at."

When the door closed behind him, Maury came to my side at the bar and put his arm about my shoulders. "He's no more unhappy than you were, you know. He'll get over it."

"Maury, is there anyone you know who hasn't fucked up his life real good?"

He shook his head.

"What do you think is going to happen?"

"I think Jason was right, all the way. I don't know how long the Vietnam war is going to drag out, but after it's over—and it will end, they all do eventually—it's going to be ugly. Use the key, Emily, if you have to. Promise?"

I pressed his hand on my shoulder. "Promise."

"He really isn't mine, is he? I know, you told me his birthdate and how much he weighed in and all that. But there's no official record, you know."

I kissed his cheek. "No, Maury. He isn't."

He sighed and put his glass down and returned to the chair. "I wish he were," he said. "I'd give anything I own if he were."

"What is it, Maury? What's wrong?"

"The whole world seems wrong somehow," he said wearily. "Kennedy, now the war, an egomaniacal president. It's all gone sour."

"And you're really afraid "

"Yes. I keep coming back to Jason's book. What a damn shame no one ever published it. He'd be rediscovered now, a whole cult would rise around him and his prophecies. I'd be a high priest of the cult. A real Jeremiah."

I sat on the arm of his chair. He held me and I put my cheek on his head. "Remember my panic of ten years ago, Maury? You said I had glimpsed mortality. It was more than that, wasn't it? You're glimpsing now what I saw then."

"I've been a fool all my life, haven't I? You've seen me busting my ass for this and that, and all the while you knew it was cotton candy, all of it. Now I know it, too, and I wonder what it's all for. The cabin isn't really for us, you know. I think we'll live out our lives in the cotton-candy world, but when it collapses, Scotty will need a place to run to. I hope he keeps his key, remembers this is here. I can do that much for him, even if he isn't mine."

I kissed his forehead, and we remained close, comforting each other until we heard Scotty on the porch, making plenty of noise to warn us of his approach. Scotty made dinner and we played poker that night and Maury lost four dollars to my son and complained bitterly about it.

Now perhaps the time is coming nearer when we shall want to use the cabin. Scotty asked me only last summer, smiling to show that he was not altogether serious, if I still had my key. "Keep it in a safe place," he said. Then he left, first for England, then the Azores, then the bottom of the sea. He sent me a card from Stonehenge. I hope he saw Stonehenge in the rain.

"We're through," Jason said. "For two days we're on our own, then back home. Where should we go? I'd like to see Stonehenge."

"Let's get lost on the moors and never let them find us!"

"I'll arrange transportation, an inn. Can you leave today, this afternoon?"

It was raining. We watched water hieroglyphics on the train windows. We held hands and didn't talk in the overcrowded compartment. The inn was filled with RAF officers on leave. They were cheerful and very young. At dinner Jason watched them broodingly; we were both subdued and it seemed that our outing had been a miserable mistake. I could hear the driving rain. Across the hall in the public bar, someone began to play jazz on a piano. It sounded very far away.

"After dinner, let's listen," Jason said, his mood changed. He glanced about the room, exposed beams, white walls, a large fireplace with a log blazing. "This must be a renovated manor house. Did you notice all the wings? It goes off in all directions. We don't need moors. We could get lost in here. It's a spiderweb inn."

"Jason, let me go home with you."

He smiled at me and covered my hand with his. "Are you game for a hike in the rain if it doesn't let up?" The waiter brought our food. When he left, Jason said, "We had a boy from Portuguese East Africa in one of my history classes. He was going to go home to start a school of his own, bring his people out of the past and into the twentieth century, after they drove the Portuguese out. That was his ambition. We argued a lot about it. I held that exchanging one set of shamans for another wouldn't matter in the long run."

"And just let the people live with fear and poverty forever?"

He patted my hand. "What he planned to do was destroy faith and he didn't have anything better to put in its place. He had medicines and road plans and sanitation programs. No faith."

"Giving them a few of the real necessities doesn't have to destroy their religion."

He nodded. "It does. To have faith means you believe your leaders are able in some way to make your life better, either now or after death. It doesn't necessarily mean *you* have to have unshakable faith personally, and most people never know if they do or not because it's never tested. But you have to believe your leaders can be mediators between you and God, or gods. Whenever the people realize their leaders don't have faith any longer, they get rid of them. As long as they think they do, they support them and add to their power with this support. If technology undermines the witch doctors, they will be abandoned and faith will die. There will be no mediator then. It is the mediator that keeps chaos at bay. Royalty served as mediator, Catholicism did, Protestantism, nationalistic governments of various colors and stripes, industrialization; none of them lasted, but each was supreme at one time. We'll go to technology and science when we decide our government has lost faith. Eventually we'll run out of people or groups, and there will be chaos."

"I don't understand what you're getting at. Are you saying people shouldn't believe in their government?"

"Look at him," Jason said, inclining his head. I turned and looked at the boy he was studying. Twenty, no more than that, he was blond and fair, with bright blue eyes. "He's willing to die because he believes his government has faith in itself. Hitler's only strength is the belief of the German people. What if they had laughed at him? What if his armies had laughed at him? They didn't and can't because they believe. When he fails them they'll have to find someone else, or something else, to become intermediary—or each one will have to acquire faith personally, individually, and that is too terrifying to consider."

"I should think it would be comforting, not terrifying."

He shook his head and said gravely, "To have the faith of Jesus would require one to live like Jesus. A scientist with absolute faith in his work is oblivious to all else. Faith absorbs the faithful, consumes them, leaves no time for anything else. Better to let the leaders walk that lonely path and support them than to go down it oneself."

"Your African friend, did he carry out his ambition? Bring education to the masses?"

"No. He was killed by a drunk driver during his senior year."

We didn't go to bed until very late. We listened to the jazz musician, then talked to the young officers a long time, and drank too much Scotch, then had sandwiches, and finally went to our room. We made love until dawn. The rain stopped and a pale sunrise painted the moors violet-gray.

"Why can't I come home with you?"

"Sh. Let's sleep for four hours and then take our hike."

"I love you, Jason. I want to marry you and take care of you. You're so thin, and you don't eat when you should, and you work too hard. You need someone to take care of you."

"Sh."

"You do love me. I can tell you love me."

"Yes, I love you very much."

"Is it because of Maury? Do you want me to tell you about Maury and me?"

"No. I understand about you and Farber. You can trust him and he can trust you. That's enough. Don't cry, Emily."

"I'm not crying. I'm drunk. I've never told anyone I wanted to take care of him before. I never loved anyone like this before. I never proposed to anyone before."

"Later, Emily. I have to do something first. I have to get rid of the devil first."

I held him tighter and denied his devil.

"For someone who isn't crying you are leaking a lot," he said, wiping his chest on the sheet. "Listen a minute. When I look in the mirror sometimes, I don't see me at all, I see my father. He has started to take little girls' clothes off to examine them. God tells him to do it. And he has a mastery of profanity that is astounding, considering that he never used that sort of language in his life. God's voice in his ear. And sometimes, when I'm working hard, my hand starts to write strange things that I can't be responsible for. Things I don't know about. The devil in me. Sometimes I see things I can't even describe because there aren't any words."

His voice was dead, there was a fixed smile on his face, and the room had become ice cold.

"But not when you're with me! Let me help you!"

His arm tightened around me and he kissed my cheek. "How flushed you look. Sex is very good for you. You should always have a man to love you. It would be criminal for you to deny yourself out of a misplaced sense of morality. Never let yourself be conned into behaving in a way that can't possibly do anyone else any good and can only do you harm."

I withdrew from his arms and lay on my back, staring at the ceiling. "If we're going to walk to Stonehenge today, we should sleep if possible. It's about four miles."

He rolled over and put his hand on my breast and closed his eyes. A few minutes later the rain started again.

A month later Maury wrote to tell me Jason had killed himself, they were hushing it up, claiming poor health, and what a damn shame it all was. I was pregnant.

That's your father, I should say to Scotty. Crazy, you know. He shot himself in the head. He heard voices and saw things that weren't there. His father was crazy, too. And possibly before him there was another crazy one. I should say that to Scotty. He doesn't believe me about Leslie Scott, maybe he never has believed it. Maybe there was something in my voice, something in the way I said it, something someone else said to instill doubt. Sometimes I see him examining Maury with speculative eyes, as if comparing his own features with Maury's and finding it not impossible.

I stood on a bridge staring into the waters below for hours and remembered Jason's story about the man whose teeth were pulled. I understood why he hadn't simply jumped; there were things to be considered first. In the end I turned and walked home again.

Years after he served in Vietnam as a technical advisor, Scotty told me that he had believed at the time he was doing the right thing, that the government was correct in its actions, that our motives for the war were beyond question, that he was morally certain that the course of the war was justified. He said all this with a cynicism that was more dismaying than his earlier beliefs.

That was what Jason had meant, a loss of belief in the faith of those whom one has allowed to rule, with nothing better to replace it. Cynicism, withdrawal, chaos. And Scotty asked me if I still had my key to the mountain cabin.

I wonder if Scotty can find his salvation in science, in his search for the well of creation at the bottom of the sea. I hope so, but I don't think he will find anything. He and his team are following orders, not striking out a lonely path by themselves. And the leader, the one with unshakable faith, is alone, I am certain, not part of a group with group-think dictating to them.

You don't need the moors in order to get lost, or a spiderweb inn, or a rambling house high on a hill overlooking a beautiful city. The worst way of being lost is to wander alone in one's own head and find that there is no exit. There comes a time when the hands and body are stilled, when there is nothing one can do, and then follows the realization that one is hopelessly lost, has been lost for a very long time, and the long trail one has carved has long since joined itself to form a circle.

13

"God damn it! Do you always have to take the most unpopular position?" The colonel glowered at me across the bed, the magazine open to the latest article by Burt Valente. It was about oil and the energy crisis and the rape of the land that would follow inevitably.

"What do you object to about it?"

"The tone, the content, the research, the conclusions."

"Besides all that, you really liked it fine, right?"

He didn't relax.

"Colonel, Burt has done his homework. He has documentation for everything."

"There's a passel of conservation magazines already. Either they're subsidized or they go down the tube. You know that."

"You don't even own the magazine any longer, why are you going into this?"

"Because I know what it means to you. If you deliberately wanted to destroy it, and your place in it, you couldn't find a quicker way."

He is so old, I thought with pity. So very old and helpless, relying on his daughter for everything. He was bedridden most of the time, propped up with pillows, too weak to sit in a chair, and the left side of his face was paralyzed, the result of a stroke two years earlier. I don't want that to happen, I heard myself saying deep inside. I'll take the bridge first. His face had always been so animated, and now it was grotesque.

"Emily, listen to me. I know, and you should, that you can't buck the money boys, no way, and stay in business. They'll stomp you down into the ground. Maybe not immediately, that would be crude, but it won't be too long either. You're controversial, always have been, but now you're treading on sore toes and the people you're hurting have the power. All the power, honey."

His speech was very slow, precise as always, but with pauses between words, as if he had to search around for the right ones, recall consciously how to shape them before he could use them.

"Colonel, there always are people with power ready to bring down anyone who crosses them. Remember the witch hunters? We weathered it. It got pretty rough, but we managed. I made the round of advertisers personally, remember, and persuaded many of them to stick with us, and told the others to fuck off. You can't just bow down and genuflect when they make a fist. Or you might as well be dead."

"We haven't seen such power on this earth since the heyday of the Roman Catholic Church," he said with agonizing slowness. "The Church set the standard for right and wrong, good and bad; they had the power to make the laws and enforce them and punish the law breakers, but they were out in the open, there was no doubt about who was doing what to whom. Nothing's in the open now, but the power is just as concentrated. They'll smash you, Emily. Back off."

I shook my head. "Burt has three more in this series, they are brilliant and deserve publication. He'd get them published in one of the other magazines, the conservation magazines, if I don't do them."

"But they can be discounted there," the colonel said. "Another nut piece. You are giving him the stamp of authority. I don't think you realize the prestige you give your writers by publishing them. It's the difference between being published in a movie fan magazine and the *New York Times*. When you publish a Maurice Farber article, it gets picked up and reprinted everywhere, it's quoted, read, and discussed. The circulation isn't large, but it circulates where it counts. Do you realize that, Emily? You turned into a hell of an editor," the colonel said. "A hell of an editor, but you're going to get hurt. You're bucking the wrong people now." He groped for my hand, patted it awkwardly. "Do you know what you're doing? Really know?"

"I have the feeling I'm adrift in the sea," I said then, voicing my deepest fears. "Every time I think I can see something to cling to, it turns out to be part of an octopus, and it's going to take me under. Take everyone under with it. And I don't know what to do about it."

He shook his head. The left side of his face was so peaceful, the eye gazing into space without fear or doubt. The other side twisted as he struggled with his words. "You can't do anything, Emily. No one can. We keep thinking we can change something, but we can't. You stir the surface of the waters now and then, make a few ripples that people mistake for waves, but when they smooth out again, nothing's been changed."

His daughter came in to hint that I was outstaying my time. He scowled at her, but didn't protest. I leaned over and kissed his dry cheek. "I'll go down," I said. "I know that, but, by God, I'll take me a piece or two of octopus along."

He laughed, but his good eye was watery when I turned to leave him. We've lived too long, Colonel, you and I. We've seen too much, know too much, and they can't make us believe any longer that change is progress and essentially good. I'm glad he doesn't know about the magazine now, glad he can't understand what happened one year after he said it would; even though he knew it would happen, as long as it was in the future, there was always the possibility of a miracle. He's out of it. The miracle has not turned to ashes for him.

I wonder if Jason foresaw this, too. I can't remember. He knew we would worship at the altar of science and technology, and he knew we would find them unworthy mediators and abandon them, but did he see anything replacing them? Jackie Wonder is a suction cup of the octopus that threatens to smother the earth.

Scotty and I sat on a fishing pier at twilight, the memory of a flamboyant sunset still persisting like an afterimage in my mind. Scotty had caught a small octopus and was using it for bait. He was intent on his line, on the restless water that rose and fell soundlessly. A movement in my peripheral field distracted me and I turned to see one of the octopus legs creeping on the bench; I froze in horror. Scotty had cut off the tentacles and they were moving, seeking the ocean once more. Down the side of the bench a second one was moving, much as an inchworm does, thrusting itself out, pulling the back section up after the front, thrusting out again.

I backed away in revulsion. "Scotty, look!"

He glanced down and then propped his rod against the rail to watch the legs creeping toward the sea. When one got near the edge of the pier he picked it up and returned it to the bench. Over and over he frustrated their efforts to escape. How long this went on I didn't know. I stared at the pieces of octopus and my son, who had become a monster to me, and I felt cold and numb. Suddenly Scotty knocked one of the legs off the pier, then picked up one he had only a moment earlier put on the bench and threw it out into the sea. He had to pull two of them loose from where they clung to the boards and he became more frenzied in his attempt to return them all to the ocean. He was flushed and angry-looking when he finished.

He searched the smooth surface of the water, which hid everything, then turned to me, and for a long time we looked at each other without speaking. His flush faded and the tension left his face. From below us the water boiled suddenly and we looked, but there was nothing to see, only the after effects, which were already being lost on the immensity of the ocean's surface. The ripples smoothed out as we watched.

Scotty nodded once, then sat down, picked up his rod, and continued to fish. Neither of us ever mentioned that evening. But something had communicated between us, something important, something neither of us could have articulated, I am certain.

That was one of the stepping stones that Maury talked about in a book. Lives are built around stepping stones, incidents that remain unchanged in the memory yet somehow change the person. When we talked about it, he said, "You were an early stepping stone, Emily. When I realized what the law could do to you, I knew I couldn't stay on that side of it. I had to get out and try to change it from a different place. I thought I was going to be able to change something when I went to work for FDR's team. Then I saw that that was hopeless, and I had to get out of that too. The stepping stone there was the night I accepted that we would indeed enter the war, that if no excuse presented itself, one would be found. No one said that to me, but suddenly I knew it. I was at dinner with Estelle and Margaret, and I understood as if a private film had been played before my inner eye. The next week, on Wednesday, I handed in my resignation. I can remember every detail of that dinner. Just as I remember every detail of the day I met you, that silly white dress, your prim hairdo, the ragged flowers on the table. Everything."

He sympathized with some of the young idealistic men who were caught up in the Nixon scandals. "If something like this had happened in the early Roosevelt years," he said, "I'd have been in the same position. My God, such belief in a person, a personal set of ideas, a goal, it's worth the fall later just to have believed like that for a time, to know one is capable of such belief."

"At the time you wouldn't have said that. You were pretty bitter."

"At the time," he agreed. "There is no pain like the pain of disillusionment, it hurts in a place no other pain can reach, and it stays there so long. But it's been a long time, and I haven't believed in anything like that again. It left a blank space that is oppressively empty."

"Poor Maury," I murmured as facetiously as I could. I didn't like talking about blank spaces.

"Poor everybody," he said. "At least I know the source of that formless anxiety that everyone suffers from, and that's something."

"Everyone?"

"Tell me who is exempt."

I couldn't name anyone. I should have said Kenneth. He never thinks about anything, but simply is a conduit for the world of visual impressions. His photographs tell us things about the world we never would have seen for ourselves, but Kenneth feels no anxiety. He has faith in his work, one of the few people I know with real sustaining faith to fill that hollow oppressive blank.

I don't want to think about blank spaces at all, no more now than I did when Maury talked about it and I kept changing the subject.

Stepping stones. Meeting Louis was a stepping stone in my life. It was at a dance at Janet Buckthorn's house.

Janet's mother introduced us and saw us on our way to the dance floor, where we both felt awkward and out of place, forced on each other like consolation prizes. Louis had been trying to dance with Janet all evening, and she kept avoiding him, and I had stood for an hour with a frozen smile because I knew no one there except Janet, and I was afraid of them all.

"Are you a school friend of Janet's?" Louis asked, searching for her all the time.

"Yes. We'll graduate together."

It was my turn and there was nothing to say, nothing I wanted to ask him, nothing I wanted to hear from him, nothing I wanted to tell him about me. He was shy and looked more like twenty than twenty-six, and he was painfully in love with Janet. I wanted only to end the dance and hide somewhere until Janet's brother appeared to escort me back to the women's dormitory at school.

Someone bumped us and Louis apologized.

"It wasn't your fault." I was too sharp. In desperation I asked, "Do you live here? In New York?"

"For now. I work here, but my home is in San Francisco."

I stopped dancing. "Me too!"

"You're from San Francisco? Where?"

"Russian Hill. You?"

"Telegraph Hill." He danced me off the floor. "May I bring you some punch?"

We didn't dance much after that. Later we gave it up altogether. He never was a good dancer and never liked trying; he was awkward on the floor until we separated. I used to wonder if his second wife ever taught him to enjoy it.

We talked about San Francisco, restaurants, favorite spots, playing on the wharves, mutual friends and acquaintances. Eventually Mrs. Buckthorn was drawn to us, this time with the intent to rend asunder what she had joined.

"Louis! You're being unfair, monopolizing Emily like this. Come dear, there is someone else I want you to meet."

"Oh, we were just going to have something to eat," Louis said. Then to me, "You go on, but come back in a quarter of an hour, over by those tables, and I'll have a plate waiting for you."

I glanced from him to Mrs. Buckthorn and suppressed a giggle. "Thank you, Mr. Carmichael. Fifteen minutes."

"I wouldn't dream of interrupting your supper," Mrs. Buckthorn protested. "I'll find you later, dear." She left.

Several times that evening I caught her watching us. I began to feel uncomfortable, as if she suspected me of trying to steal her silverware.

"She intended for us to amuse each other for a little while," Louis said, dismissing her. "She didn't intend for us to get along so well. She probably thinks I'm too old for you."

I laughed. He was so ill at ease at the party, homesick, desperate for someone to talk to about home; if he was dangerous, I was Mata Hari. It never occurred to me that Mrs. Buckthorn was concerned for Louis, that in the club in which both families were members, there was a mutual unspoken agreement to protect the offspring from outsiders.

Did I love him? I have come back to that a hundred times. When we were driven apart, I wanted to die. Now I think it must have been a combination of many different reasons. We discovered sex together. Louis wasn't a virgin, but his experiences had been with prostitutes, whom he regarded with repugnance and the twin fears of discovery and disease. Until I married him, I never had been really alone in my adult life. Young women were not allowed to leave the school alone; we were always in groups with a chaperon. The new freedom was exhilarating. And we seemed rich. Louis had no money of his own yet, he didn't inherit until he was thirty, but his pay and mine seemed all the money in the world. Later, when I was poor, hungry, and alone, I could look back on those months as exciting, rich, and happy. But did I love him? I don't know.

If they had given us time, we would have found out. But as it is, I'll never know, Louis will never know, and he will declare his undying love now with sincerity, believing every word to be true.

How few of the people I know have been willing to come into this year. Louis is living his youth once more. Randolf, my brother, is living his childhood in my house; Wanda, my sister, is living twenty years ago. They all stopped along the way. Even Tony would rather back up than go forward. And Maury, so disillusioned, so cynical now, he is keeping pace, but with an eye that sees too deeply, past the surface, to find the skeleton of truth that may be beautiful to an anatomist, but not to anyone else. Perhaps he is the only realist among us.

It occurs to me that I might have been trapped here all night and a day or two days, or more. If the house fell in such a way that no light gets to me, there is no way I can tell. I am thirsty, and light-headed, and the shadows that dance in and out of my mind are gathering about me in a great circle that pulses in and out. I know that I dare not fall asleep again, or they will move closer and closer; slowly, testing their power, but inexorably, they will move in until they touch me, and then collapse in on me from all directions and I'll become a shadow also.

It annoys me that this might give satisfaction to some people I wouldn't bother to throw a rope to if they were sinking. Claudia Ess, for example. She told malicious lies about me, oh, ten, fifteen years ago. She will smile sadly at Scotty, pat his hand. Estelle has every reason to hate me; she might rejoice. But Estelle is in the hospital herself, and she is too lazy to be affected one way or the other. She would rather suffer in silence than protest my existence, or take pleasure in my passing; she is paving her way to heaven with suffering. There is Maude Lange, who thinks she would have Kenneth if I dropped dead. She is wrong. Kenneth likes to photograph her because she is as beautiful as a sunset, as beautiful as a bird in flight, as beautiful as a tree in its prime of life with no disease or insects to ravage it, and he thinks of her in much the same way he thinks of those other natural wonders. There are all those people who wanted jobs that I couldn't provide. All those people who wanted to be published whom I disappointed. There are those we exposed in articles—politicians, businessmen, artists of all sorts, performers. . . . There is Gregory Ludlow, who thinks I stole some story ideas and gave them to my friends to write. I told him to sue for damages if he was so certain, but he wouldn't do that, and he simply talked about it until I threatened to sue him. He knows what he knows, and nothing will ever shake that.

There is Scotty. I recoil from the thought, but there he is among the others. Scotty isn't an enemy. Scotty is just confused and unhappy and has a tendency to blame it all on me. And perhaps he is convinced that he will not be allowed to find happiness until I am dead, but even that does not make him hate me. It is the dark irrational part of his mind that is still eight or nine years old that screams out, I hate you! It's all your fault!

He came into the living room, where Kenneth was photographing Homer with a can of beer in his hand, his messy manuscript scattered on the floor about him. "What the hell are you doing?"

Kenneth glanced toward him, then returned to his camera. "Be done in a minute," he said absently.

"Why is it always like this?" Scotty demanded of me when I came up behind him. "It doesn't matter when I come home, it's like this!"

"Come into the other room," I said as soothingly as I could manage. "How long will you be here?"

"I'm not staying! I can't stay in this madhouse! You make it impossible for me to come home at all!"

We stood in the hall. Karen and Katherine came running downstairs laughing, on their way to classes. "See you later, Aunt Emily," one of them called at the outside door. "Hi, Scotty!" the other yelled, and they swept out.

"How can you stand it all the time?"

"It's home like this. Would you want me to live in this great house all by myself?"

"Sell the goddamn house and get an apartment! As long as you have it you'll think you have to keep it filled!"

"What's wrong, Scotty? What's happened?" He looked miserable.

The living-room door opened and Kenneth struggled out with his equipment. "That damn Indian is being so Indian chief I can't get a thing. Why does he revert to that every time I get near him with a camera?"

"He wants posterity to see him the way he chooses, not the way you choose," I said.

Scotty looked from one to the other of us, then said to Kenneth, "Why don't you clear out of here? Why are you always hanging around?"

"Scotty! That's none of your business!"

Kenneth hardly seemed to notice the outburst. He was taking his camera off the tripod, muttering about Homer and his poses. Scotty took a step closer to him and I grabbed his arm.

"If you want to see me, come on upstairs, or into the study. I don't want to stand in the hallway." I started for the stairs and after a moment he followed.

He wouldn't sit down. "This has to stop, Mother!" he

said. "It is driving me crazy seeing you live this kind of life!"

I turned to the drapes and opened them, trying to still laughter. "Yes," I said, not looking at him. "Go on."

"I want you to live like other people's mothers. You're too old to have this much going on all the time. It worries me."

"Scott, what's really on your mind?" I sat down then and waited.

He stood stiffly, awkward in my room, self-conscious and unhappy. "I've been going to a psychiatrist," he said. "He says I should talk to you, get to know you better, tell you what I think."

"And that's what you think. I should be like other people's mothers."

"Yes! I'm . . . I'm ashamed of you."

"Why?"

"Why? Why? You ask me why? If you don't know that much how can I even talk to you? Mother, have you ever thought maybe you need help? Hasn't it occurred to you that if you're so out of step with the world, maybe the world isn't sick, maybe it's you!"

"Scotty, for heaven's sake, sit down. You give me the jeebies looming over me like that. I'm not sick. I never said the whole world was wrong, or sick, or anything else. And what makes you think I'm that different from other people? Isn't Cissy living alone, working? There are a lot of women who are single, support themselves, don't live like nuns in a retreat."

"But they don't surround themselves with lovers either!"

He blanched and clutched the back of the sofa, then abruptly turned and went to the window, where he stood with his back to me.

Finally it was in the open, finally after twenty years, and there was nothing I could say to him, nothing I could do for him. I wanted to hold him in my arms and soothe him, tell him I loved no one as much as I loved him, tell him the men in the house were not my lovers. And, of course, I could do none of those things. "Scotty, you are hurt, I know, but I haven't done it to you. I've never done anything to hurt you, Scotty. When it was time to let you go, I did, but you haven't let go yet, honey. You're still demanding, insisting on molding me into an image that never existed outside your mind. It won't work, Scotty. You can't do it."

"I told him it wouldn't do any good," Scotty muttered. "No point in any of this, never was." He left the window, walking as carefully as a drunk before a judge. "Mother, I have to go. What I really came for is to ask you if you'll move into an apartment on the East Coast somewhere. I'm making a lot of money now and I could pay your rent without any trouble. You could give up working, retire. Will you think about it?"

"I was shaking my head before he finished. "Your psychiatrist didn't suggest that."

"No. It's my idea. I didn't mention it to him."

"Thank you, honey. But no thanks. What you don't realize, what no one seem to realize, is that I work because I love my work, not because I have to. Although I do have to, but that's secondary. And I love this house and having people here, working with them, watching them develop into something else. What in God's name would I do in an apartment?"

He wasn't listening. Slowly he looked about my room, his gaze lingering on the bed, and when he looked again at me, I felt a stranger had slipped into his shoes.

"I'll go now," he said. "I'm sorry I interrupted you."

"Scotty, wait! You know you don't interrupt me. I love for you to come."

He nodded, then left without looking at me again.

When he called me to say he was up from the sea floor there wasn't any indication that he had had his talk with me. Nothing had changed. And that day in my room, I had seen hatred and frustration and shame and I don't know what else all mixed together in one mask come down over his face when he looked at me that last time. His face had been a stranger's face that day.

If I were dead he would be able to admit to a certain admiration and affection. "She was a great old girl," he could say then, and mean it. Now, he is filled with anguish because of me.

I heard something. Something . . . No it is gone. Only the surf sounds and the pulse in my neck, in my ears, nothing else. Perhaps there was a rumble of an aftershock after all this time. I wanted to think of why we stay here, those of us who know there will be another major quake, who know the city will be destroyed, just as surely as

Pompeii, as ancient Crete, which might have been Atlantis of Plato's *Timaeus*.

"I wish a tidal wave would come!" Scotty used to say, standing at the edge of the sea, staring across the waters. And in the mountains: "I wish a volcano would blow up!"

"I wish an earthquake would come," Wanda and I used to say, overlooking the city, imagining the havoc, seeing the buildings crumble into dust.

We are forced to bury such wishes. To desire catastrophe is neurotic insane, taboo. It is to welcome death on such a scale that all our heroic efforts must fail, and we cannot admit thoughts that border on madness and that treat death as anything but the enemy. The colonel made his daughter promise not to hospitalize him, to permit him to die at home, in his bed. But the doctors and the law will prevail because it is sane and moral to deny death at any cost.

Yet we flock to the sea coasts where hurricanes threaten; we crowd into doomed cities like San Francisco; we dance on the bottom of the sea and climb the highest mountains. And there is the contradition that imposes its penalty on each of us; that is the stress that splits us into the surface rationality that mouths phrases like death is the enemy; and that other, deeper, less rational part that courts death.

In our fear of death we dance at the lip of the volcano, play with doomsday weapons, flaunt our susceptibility to disease by discovering and manufacturing new diseases in our laboratories, invent heroic measures to postpone death even after the patient has accepted it. We turn our world into a valley of death where we must walk gingerly, for death bubbles up here, there, like eruptions in a seething mud flat, and life is spent waiting for the next holocaust.

We will not be driven away from the fault lines and the storm belts because we welcome signs that the power of the earth will prevail, that man's efforts will be put into perspective, that there are greater forces than we can control, that the petty changes we bring about at such cost to ourselves are in the end as nothing. Our helplessness is finally justified. Such acceptance allows a peace that the shifting theories of science and the ceaseless exhortations and promises of theology and ideology can only hint at.

14

"Mrs. Carmichael!" A real voice? I strain to hear it better. It is distant and indistinct. Father? Of course not. When he comes he sits within reach, and brings the fragrance of woods and earth, and his voice is loud and clear, not like this phantom voice that blends with the surf.

"If you can hear me, Mrs. Carmichael, don't try to move, but try to call out. I'll count to three, then wait for your answer. One, two, three."

I try to make a sound; it is smothered in the mattress. I don't move a muscle, but then I haven't moved a muscle for hours, or days, or however long this has been. Now there is only the silence again, and it might have been the surf, breaking through formlessness into speech after all this time.

"Tony! Can you see? Are people here now, digging me out?"

"Emily, you have to let me take you home after this. You could have been killed. Next time you won't be so lucky."

His voice is rough with fear. Whose fear, Tony? Yours? At the thought of death so close to you once more?

"This is hardly the time to be talking like that," I say.

"Until I'm above ground such talk certainly seems a bit premature."

"What will you do, damnit? You don't have any money! You don't have a job! What in hell do you think you can do now? Go back to that madhouse and just wait for the earthquake that will kill you?"

"Yes. If I can."

Tony is a good businessman. He puts first things first. Maury does to a certain extent, possibly not as automatically as Tony, but enough to make certain that his retarded daughter will never be neglected, enough to make certain that Estelle will have the proper care now, enough to know he'll always have a home. The gene that causes geology to erupt must also cause poverty to happen late in life. My grandfather, my father, now me.

"Tony?" There is no answer. I suppose I made him angry again. I don't really think I am good for Tony. I make him lose his temper more than anyone else, or anything else. He might develop high blood pressure with me, have a heart attack, or a stroke. He would insist that I be called Mrs. Kodel. He would set about creating a new woman who would fit his image of what Mrs. Kodel should be, and that new woman would most certainly erase Emily Carmichael right out of the picture.

". . . equipment. We have a doctor here, and an ambulance on the way. . . ."

Either someone is up there calling to me, or the surf has been bewitched.

"Honey, how are you doing?"

"Father! I have to ask you. Were you happy? Was your life good?"

He sits at the foot of my bed; I sit crosslegged at the other end and we regard each other. There are bits of dry pine needles in his hair and the fragrance of forests enclouds us.

"Happy?" He seems puzzled by the word, repeating it again several times, frowning in deliberation, as if hearing it for the first time. Finally he says, "Sometimes. Sometimes not. It was a good life, though."

"I wanted Scotty to be happy. That was my prayer for him, my only prayer for him. It was wrong, wasn't it?"

"It isn't something you can go out and find, like plucking an apple off a tree," Father says. "It's more like something that sneaks up on you when you least expect it, when you're too busy to know it's been somehwere else until then."

"I've failed him," I say, and ease myself back down between the bed and the chaise, where I belong. "I tried and failed him."

"I failed you, honey. You and Randolf and Wanda, your mother. I failed you all."

"But you didn't! My life has been good! There has been a great deal of happiness, more than I've ever deserved! You didn't fail us!'

He laughs, and his laughter blends into the sounds of the sea and the sounds of something else that I can't identify. Digging.

There is something else I want to tell my father. "Wait," I call out to him. "Come back."

"Now what?" He sounds as he used to when I called him back to my bedside for the second or third time.

"Father, listen a minute. I just found out something." I examine his face. "You probably already know and you'll laugh at me, but that's all right."

"Is it something silly then?"

"Yes. So silly and so simple I can't imagine why it's a secret." Although nothing of it shows on his face, he is laughing inside. I remember sitting on his lap and feeling his laughter shake me. "I'm still me," I say. "I'm still Emily, me. When I was little I thought when I grew up I'd be someone else. When I was thirty, I thought by forty I'd be someone else. But it never happened. I'm still me!"

He laughs aloud, and laughing, clasps me tight against him for a moment. "I know. I know."

I'm still me, I repeat again, alone now, not quite laughing, but almost. I'm still me!

They *are* digging up there.

They have brought a grader of some sort, something to push the earth back into a flat place where they can build another house. Mr. Rossiter must have hired them to level it again.

"Get me out of here first, you bastards! Don't you dare build a house on top of me!"

They can't hear me. I hope there are no television people out there, no photographers. My hair must be every which way, and I'm wearing this old granny gown made of flannel that is soft and faded from many years of good usage. Dorrie has tried hard to keep me looking proper and well dressed, but I like this old gown and now I'll probably see it all over the scandal sheets, the tabloids. Old woman saved from earthquake in thrity-year-old gown.

At least my teeth are all mine. I won't blink in the light of day and smile to expose my gums, and later find my teeth shattered in a glass somewhere.

I imagine Dorrie has money saved, wisely invested. She always listened to Maury with attentiveness. She thinks Maury is the smartest, wisest, nicest man who's ever been in my life. She could be right.

Something shifted in the house. Something heavy that made a shudder pass through the bed, through me. They are cursing, and that is strangely reassuring. I hope to God they know what they're doing. I hope they brought in people who understand graders and shovels and houses that are leaning perilously. Old woman sues rescuers for knocking house into sea. Old woman swept out to sea by rescuers. Scotty would sue them then.

I wish Father would not pop in and out like Mars swimming in and out of range through the telescope. Scotty cried, "There it is, Mother! Don't you see it?" But in and out it went, until I turned the instrument over to him in defeat. I would ask Father why his life was good. What made it a good life? But I think I know. He seized it early and never let go until he died. It was his life all the way. And he didn't burden himself with the responsibility of bringing happiness to his children. He gave us all we could absorb and then let us go. A good life.

"Mother, you must see now how foolish it is to stay here. You have to get rid of this old house. Get an apartment, out of this area altogether."

"Like the colonel did?" I ask him. "He went to New York and worked harder than ever, remember?"

The colonel. How many careers did he have? Four, five? Every time he retired he became busier than before. died and was reborn over and over.

Dorrie said, "You won't starve, and I won't either." And we made out through the years. We made out.

"Mrs. Carmichael, it won't be long now. We're nearly there now."

Again. They are playing jackstraws with the cottage beams and timbers.

I could write my memoirs, write a bestseller, retire gracefully and live on my royalties.

The house shuddered again. I can hear the machines closer, a throbbing noise that could be an engine.

I would have to have it ghosted. I could edit it, but I wouldn't be able to write anything myself.

I could lecture. There is a demand these days for successful women to appear on campuses, before clubs. I could go into politics. But I hate public speaking, and I don't like staying in hotels and eating in restaurants in strange cities.

I could run a boarding house. Or Dorrie could. I would lose a decimal a day, and the crazy zeros won't stay put. I could search for the buried gold, maybe even find it, or conduct guided tours of the house like English nobility, or learn to knit baby booties or hire out as a go-go dancer or . . .

I won't starve! And I won't lose my house! I promise myself that much and have to laugh here against the mattress. I sound like Jackie Wonder making promises he can't keep.

The house is beautifully decorated for the party. I pause at the top of the stairs and gaze down at the large room that was meant for a ballroom. Everyone I know is there; there are balloons and streamers, and a four-piece band is playing.

"Come to the party, Father," I say; and take his arm to descend the stairs. We dance the first dance together, then Homer dances with me, and Kenneth and Tony and Frank Stacy and Red, and we drink Tony's champagne, and eat Dorrie's hors d'hoeuvres, and dance some more. No one dances as well as Jason, though, and when he takes my arm I tell him this. He is pleased and we whirl about the room as one.

"You are a plant that can be put in the earth in the coldest weather," he says, laughing at me, with me, "and when spring comes, there are calluses where roots will grow. A new plant will burst forth and thrive."

I can hear gears being shifted; the cottage shudders.

Maury dances with me, not as smoothly as Jason, but it isn't fair to compare everyone else with Jason. "It was a lovely party," Maury says, and I see that my guests have gone. We dance alone in the great room to soft music from the stereo.

The cottage shifts again and now I feel a draft on my legs and they are cold; voices are close by. It is too hard to distinguish their words. I really don't care very much what they are saying. What a joke if they find me asleep. I'll swear I slept through it all.

To Maury I say, "Yes, it is a lovely party." And we dance around the great ballroom.